# Letters *from the* Void

published by Coincidence Control Publishing in Portland, OR

# LETTERS

—

# INTRODUCTION

*"The very cave you are afraid to enter turns out to be the source of what you are looking for."*

– Joseph Campbell

This book is strange. It comes to you from Portland, Oregon which, as many of its citizens can attest, is an epicenter of weirdness. More specifically, it comes from a little shop that is itself a little island of weirdness in a sea of weirdness – a curious, brightly colored little shop called Float On, which is what we call a float tank center. I am a manager of said float tank center.

A float tank is a device designed to shield a human being from environmental stimulation. This is done by placing the subject inside some kind of a sound dampening chamber, half submerged in a pool of epsom salt saturated, skin temperature water in total darkness and total silence for an extended period of time, in hopes of fomenting in them an altered state of consciousness that is both pleasing and healthy. So, yeah, the idea is a little weird.

That said, people on the fringes of society have been seeking solitude, darkness, quiet, and an overall lack of external stimulation as a means of inducing altered states of consciousness for millennia. Consider all the different monks praying silently in their dark meager monasteries, the yogi sitting in his cave up in the mountains, the kivas of the Hopi, or the Cappadocians with their massive networks of underground chambers. They're all seeking isolation and sensory deprivation.

But the first official time a more or less modern float tank was used was in the year 1954 at the National Institute of Mental Health in Bethesda, Maryland. There, a couple of scientists named John C. Lilly and Jay T. Shurley decided to submerge someone inside a giant water filled cylindrical chamber that looked like it could just as easily be desigened for torture as for scientific research. The purpose of the experiment was to observe whether a mind would continue to produce subjective experiences once it was fully cut off from external sensory input.

The subjects of course felt a variety of negative emotions at the onset, most notably fear of drowning or asphyxiation. But, as they got more used to the sensation (or lack of) of floating suspended in total darkness and total silence, unable to even feel the water against their skin, a strange thing occurred. The fear faded and passed and gave way to a sense of peace, comfort and euphoria. In some instances the darkness and silence became punctuated by strange and dreamlike internal experiences as shapes, colors, sounds, emotions, memories, and visions bubbled up from the depths of the psyche to the surface of cognition. Some of these experiences were very profound and meaningful to the subjects. The scientists knew they were on to something.

60 years later in the city of Portland Oregon, I haphazardly decided to follow in their footsteps, and find some subjects of my own to put inside of float tanks and see what happened. This time, I chose local writers as our guinea pigs.

I did not give the writers many guidelines or rules to follow, I just asked that the writings have something to do with the float experience. Each writer floated four times and wrote a piece after each float. After about 3 years of collecting writings, I got together with my co-editor Sione Aeschliman and we picked our favorite pieces to go into this anthology.

The results were strange, fascinating, beautiful, funny, heartbreaking, uplifting, inspiring and so many other things. The works are as diverse as the people who created them, yet there are themes running throughout showing a vague but present universality at the core of the experiences as if to prove that deep, deep down, people are all the same.

We all, but writers especially perhaps, are familiar with the distinction between who we are on the surface, and who we are underneath. When one enters into a float tank, they have no choice but to confront their inner, deeper selves. The writers in this book each plumbed the depths of their being inside the float tank, they pulled back the layers, tried to get to the core of who and what they are, and then came back to write about it, each in their own unique style.

There is a loose order to this book based on the different stages of the float experience. It dawned on me while writing this introduction that the different "sections" of the book correlate quite nicely with the archetypal stages of Joseph Campbell's Hero's Journey, much to my literary satisfaction.

The first part of the book is all about The Departure. Most of these pieces were written after the first float, while our heroes were in the process of learning how to "let go." There is struggle and apprehension of doing something strange and unfamiliar, but also the pleasure and excitement of learning to leave the clamorous modern world behind, to break out of one's comfort zone, to shed one's burdens and preconceptions, and dive into the unknown.

By the middle of the book, our writers are fully immersed in the float experience and off on their own private vision quests through the dreamscapes of their minds. They have descended Into the Underworld. Quite often during a float the mind comes to point where it loses sense of orientation and rootedness in physical reality and the body. At this point our heroes may experience all manner of strange thoughts and free associations or witness sudden visual displays of colors or patterns, hear strange music, enter into a dream state, or have full-on visions of being in another place or time. It is a wonderful state for artists, musicians, poets, and writers to find creative inspiration.

The end of the book correlates to Initiation and The Return, focusing on the healing and transformative aspects of the float experience and coming back to the world again with new insight, knowledge, and optimism. This is where our heroes find the object of their quest, insofar as they even know that they were on a quest or looking for something. In the altered state of consciousness that arises as a byproduct of lack of sensory input, in the silence and darkness, and seemingly from out of nothing, they derive some profound insights and greater understandings. They heal old mental wounds, rediscover their inner strength, or gain a new outlook on the world. Somehow, the void has imparted some transformative wisdom on them, and the person who emerges from the float tank is not quite the same as the person who went in. They are still themselves, but now more so.

At the time of this writing, I have gone on almost 400 floats and I still find it nearly impossible to put words to the experience that can do it justice. Fortunately, that is not my job. Fortunately, I have these writers to do that sort of thing.

I hope you enjoy this book as much as I enjoyed helping to make it. I think the experiment turned out quite nicely in the end.

– Marshall Hammond, June 2017

# Liminality

C. Starling

noun, Anthropology.

*1. the transitional period or phase of a rite of passage, during which the participant lacks social status or rank, remains anonymous, shows obedience and humility, and follows prescribed forms of conduct, dress, etc.*

*2. the period of standing in the threshold, the moment before change, the in-between places in life*

The problem with liminal states is that they leave you vulnerable. You are no longer the self you were, and you are not yet the self you will become. Sometimes you're vulnerable for an afternoon, while you prepare to walk down the aisle and speak your vows. Sometimes you're vulnerable for a day, waiting to walk at your graduation. Sometimes you're vulnerable for months, while you wait for an answer on your book, while you wait for your house to close, while you wait to be able to take on the new identity you've crafted for yourself but can't yet claim.

The in-between places are where we become unmoored. We can't find ourselves as easily, and we become restless, uncertain, afraid. When you're on the edge of the rules that defined your past, but not yet fully protected by the laws that will suffuse your future, what happens when those rules are broken?

In Iceland, in the time of the Vikings, they knew that their laws only extended to the boundaries of their farms. In the forests between fields, you could meet a man in the darkness, and he could kill you - and the laws could not punish him. In the in-between spaces, humans can become monsters.

Crossing over a bridge, you are on neither bank. A troll might lurk beneath, hungry and waiting.

In the in-between spaces, you are vulnerable.

The darkness of the tank can be liberating, but that exact liberation, that anonymity, can be threatening. By entering the tank, you abandon everything but yourself, and yourself is not the self you know outside of the tank. The salt water and the darkness have a way of stripping you down, teaching you humility alongside a type of childlike delight. You are you inside the tank, but you are also not you. You are not the wife, the worker, the breadwinner, the maid. You are you, without labels, without definitions, without status or narrative.

And so you are vulnerable.

But vulnerability is not inherently bad. For as many times as you risk your safety, walking at the margins of the law, courting monsters and disaster, there are many more times when you come of age. When you marry your lover. When you transform yourself into the next stage of what you want to be. You can't get to a new place without passing through the darkness, through the uncertainty.

So step into the tank. Close the door.
Float in the in-between.
Say hello to yourself.

# 10 Easy Steps on How to Float Effectively

*Nikki Burian*

1

Strip yourself down to your most basic human existence. You will begin to see the outlines of vulnerabilities – this is normal. They are exposed when you are open; it has always been this way. Don't fight it yet.

2

Put your earplugs in, step inside the chamber. Close the door. Take a deep breath. Lie down.

3

Turn off the light. Keep your eyes open. What you see next is what you need.

4

You will notice how quickly insecurities come hurtling towards you in the dark. They will hover centimeters from every part of your body, waiting for you to react, hoping you will crack them open and drink their liquor worry. Insecurities are addictive. Do not swat them away, do not grab onto them. They cannot see you if you are motionless, if you ignore their allure. They will pass.

## 5

You are floating in this water not to unearth that which can destroy you, but you discover the tools necessary to keep it buried. It isn't always easy.

## 6

Fight the void you feel when you allow your senses to be stolen. Every war is different, but most are typically fought with ideas, hopes, and love. Determination is essential. Darkness is only as consuming as you make it, remember that.

## 7

What do you see when your sight is gone? What do you hear in the silence? The person you used to be waits for you in this space. They will take any and all opportunities to engulf you. They are your past for a reason. Leave them there, where they do the least harm. Visualize your ideal self shooing them away. Who you really are is present.

## 8

Find the fireworks in your peripherals and embrace them. These are the pieces of you that bring you the most joy and comfort. Allow them to explode around you. Let their light illuminate what cowers in the shadows. That is the direction you need to travel next. The next step to find your peace is over there. Walk with passion.

## 9

Reflect on how your mind kept you calm today, how it fights for that peace even in the depths of your subconscious. The battle is always worth fighting when you are in here. You are better every time you leave. Come back, fight harder.

## 10

Float on.

# First Float

*Tanya Jarvik*

At my first float, I'm left alone in the dark with a body of information, my body: winking in and out of self-awareness in the warm saltwater, floating face up, hands down. Initially, I'm a collection of minor complaints, resisting quiet, resisting rest, resisting the time this is going to take out of my day. Then, bit by bit, I allow myself to sift and settle. I surrender to the experience. I stop holding my head up. I stop keeping my legs straight. I stop surprising myself every time I swallow. I stop listening to my heartbeats, my inhales and exhales, and the faint rumble of traffic that occasionally breaks the surface of silence. Now I'm nothing but a skeleton. A concatenation of spine and vertebrae, radius and ulna, finger bones, toe bones, ilium and ischium. A skull full of stars. I'm a tiny astronaut, umbilicaled to an invisible spaceship, like the picture on the cover of my father's LP of Switched-on Bach. I'm one sustained note in a long song, a deep note. I'm a tree. Trunk, mostly, and two branches, the left one slightly bent, with a crown of feathery leaves high above the understory flora, moving in a thin wind. I'm a shark in the sea. A thanksgiving shark, shrink-wrapped in white plastic and trussed in yellow netting, grimacing on my kitchen counter, sandwiched between the fridge and the stove. My eyes snap open. Wide. A shrink-wrapped shark? I blink in blackness, considering the image. It's clearly the product of my subconscious mind, which makes me wonder whether I've been asleep, and if so, for how long. I decide it doesn't matter, and close my eyes again. Aloha.

# Can You Cheat the Void with Sleight of Hand?

*Ken Yoshikawa*


It started with Perplexus:
a spheroid puzzle game in the float shop's waiting room.
You roll a 5mm metal ball through a three-dimensional labyrinth
and stay on the track.
You learn to move the whole sphere & make gravity your friend.
Surely, though, you fail
& fail
& clang it slaps upon the plastic ramming shivers in your hands.
So you smack Perplexus back when the ball gets wedged, & you
try again & again & again & you breathe & be patient 'til all the
meditating you thought you'd done seems to fall apart & you are
frustrated.

When I laid Perplexus down,
the ball must have slid into the bones in my hand,
rolled up my arm
then right into my skull.

So when, without ado, I stepped into the void
I was not alone,

or empty,
but my hands, still obsessed with the rattle clack of failure
held my head,
as if determined to solve the puzzle of itself
and be rewarded with these neck pops all suspended,
breaking all the rules of normalcy.

Can you contend against eternity
when you can see where you end against the utter backdrop?
Can you cheat the void
with sleight of hand?

Or are you left, suspended in a block of glass,
thinking everything you do is wrong.

Your thoughts are all mistakes that wretch until there's salt inside
your eyes & then reality begins to strobe light step its way up to the
moody lighted shower head to clean itself in blue & red then turn
on back again into the dark, when even then you're still bouncing
off the walls & everything is still just wrong.
This whole thing is just a glitch, a trip, some simulation made to
flip a switch.
This doesn't change a thing about me.

But then, I breathed this fury that went down into my gut.
My body, pain, death, smell: it's all to go one day, why bother,
right?
So meaningless, this drip:
you may as well embrace it,
ride it down into the ocean, from the clouds & shattered sky,

until your toes will spark like little lightning rods.

I must have let my head go,
because the metal ball just seemed to roll right out the top.
Everything went still,
as if a lion roared.

When I moved my wrists beside my head, the ice that cased me in
would crack its lines out into space, decompressing constellations,
twisting into groans of muscle.
Bone.
The crunching noise was loud, O why so loud. The rage, this body,
cracking, spread like music meant to make you crazy.
Till the lion roared again & thunder made its quiet.

There was this drumming
distant, thumping, battle, dancing,
O & all the steady majesty, so simple, doubled
strong enduring
far beyond what any thought could ever reach.
How beautiful.

And so I gently floated on toward this beat
with wonder why my heart just feels so far away.

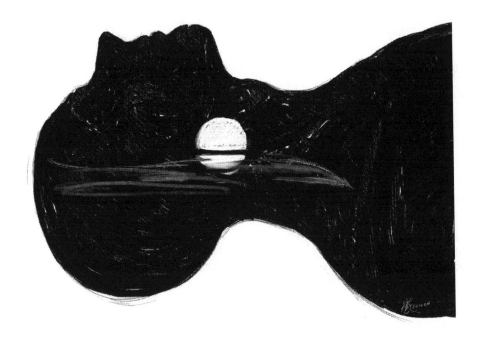

Illustration by Kathryn Sullivan

# I Ate the Moon

*Dot Hearn*

Pushing the door closed with an extra shove, as instructed, I listened to the light- and soundproof strip work its magic. With a hush and a suck and a click, the visitors' voices in the hall outside receded, locked out with the rest of the hurry and noise and bother.

I stripped off the layer of crazy clients. No, literally; I'm not exaggerating. Their stresses and troubles and acting out and. Everything. I stripped off the layers of professional, the personal, and stood naked. Listening. As the cleansing filter slowed and stopped. As the main lights were cut, leaving me. In the water room. In the light of the pool.

I showered and removed the last dust from the day. Work sliding down the drain, leaving tracks in my memory; leaving. Traces. Thoughts in motion.

The pool water was calling. A swoop, spill, splat, "come in," it said. Micro waves lapping against the 1950s turquoise walls of the tank, made louder as I stepped in. Feeling my way with warm, freshly cleaned toes. I lowered myself into the silk smooth salted water. Down. In. Now sitting. Now lying – butt, back, shoulders, head. Reclining.

Then.

I swallowed the moon and extinguished her light. Her round body rolling, smooth and bumpy, down and down until the surrounding air was dark.

A silence like the night with snow. No stars, no traffic. Head back, water over my ears. The pop on the left as an air pocket forms, releases, forms, in my ear. Now right. Hearing my heart beat in the water, in my head, in my shoulders, and the water responding. Tha-thump. Here-I-am. Tha-thump.

Warmth. Drifting, floating, touch the side, drift. Float.

I slip my body into the void of the moon. Thoughts try to follow and I let them come, wave hello, go out the other side. I curl myself in the moon's absence and look at the sky, gold stars and red planets, looking at the Earth far away in the distance. Tucked in the sphere without light, the sphere against a backdrop of velvet blackness.

Floating. I can't tell if my eyes are open. Or shut. It all looks the same.

Thoughts quiet. Become murmurs under heartbeat. Sensations shift to my water body. The moment when we meld, are one, and I no longer know where the water begins or my body ends. The moment when I don't notice breast islands, belly continent, or exposed thighs, underside of arms. I become a face breathing water hearing drifts of our heart and the moon rocks in her new home.

Warm still water strokes thump breath. Repeat. Think about poetry about story about telling vision and tasting words. Water. Thought. A few strands of hair drift to my hand tickle. Tap edge, heartbeat-inspired drift, back to center. Centered. Stillness. Wonder the time; it doesn't matter.

Notice.

Water body still whole and I ate the moon.

Notice.

Tranquility more comforting than silence.

Notice.

# In a Water of Enigmas

*Greg Elderidge*

Besotted with the idea of dispossession, Tavian disrobed, showered, and lowered himself into the pod. His body lay placid like a carcass long exiled from the fervor of living, hosting somehow an intelligence tramping rampant over derelict thoughts and ideas with a feral animosity. A comfort – he could move his fingers – a reassurance – he could wake up if he had need – and a reality check – grandma's brisket (the memory of which he time and again resorted to convince his ego of both sanity and safety): *I am okay.* He went on thus in hope of muting his own intelligence, dreaming naught but of the dream to silence at last his body and his mind. *The pod was designed to facilitate this dream,* Tavian thought, *but the dream itself cannot be dreamt while in the pod, else it never come true.* If he learned how to resign all sense of resolve, he had been told several times, then he might find silence. But he mustn't search. Only if he learned how to give up his dreams once inside might he find himself within them, they had said.

Tavian's reflections floated in a water of enigmas: How to find an answer to a question that cannot be asked? How to find a state of being he was not supposed to look for? All effort was counterproductive, and yet this itself was just another rumination thwarting his abandon of effort.

As the authority of the pod crept with scepter and crown deeper into Tavian's subconscious mind, however, he began without reserve to submit to its strange inspiration. The swarm of characters dialoging in his head cowered from their isolation from the outside world and shied away from each other as if locked for too long in the same room: the questions, paradoxes, and perplexities of a brain trying to silence itself were themselves muzzled. *Free from corporeal distraction and left on its own, the humming inside dies a peaceful decease.* This was Tavian's last articulated thought before the hallucinations began.

# Sound Waves

*Rooze Garcia*

Completely dark, I open
my eyes into another layer –
still more darkness. A play of
light against false horizon, imagined
where water meets air and memories
of glowing blue phosphorescence
blend into this illusion. I remind myself
there is nothing shining in this space
nothing externally illuminated nothing
but phantom memories hallucinated
against darkness projected by a mind
desperate for light.

~

I was wrong. It isn't
beat thump thump beat;
that elides the watery rush
pushed through valves
through veins through years.

~

This small sip of the slip
away from gravity blooms
into a desire for more. Barely
drunk, I reach for emptiness.

~

The other sound behind my heart –
what is that? What is that? What is that?
The strain of listening pushes it away.

~

I dream of vastness of spinning
untethered arms outstretched
neck tilted back, an oh
an awe, a deep breath
a yes

~

Hold my breath, the sound
persists. A desire to hush
my heart to hear more clearly.
Static. Not quite white noise.
Not quite. The rush of blood
cannot be held back.

~

A breath
and a beating heart
and a mind, difficult
to quiet, constantly

broadcasting.

~

Before the word
was the thought –
a vision of brightness
filling the void with
darkness and light.

# Breathe and Be

*Sione Aeschliman*

When Marshall said, "sensory deprivation tank," my only frame of reference was the TV show *Fringe*. I imagined being in a tight, water-filled metal coffin in total darkness, my breath echoing back at me accentuating the nearness of the walls. To someone who is claustrophobic and dreams about drowning, it sounded like dying.

I was terrified.

I needed to do it.

In truth, what convinced me more than anything was the testimonial of a friend, who assured me that if at any time I wanted to stop, I could just turn on the lights and get out. I would have control. And I figured, people do this every day and don't die. I probably won't die, either.

At Float On, Marshall ushered me down the hall and into a warm, beige-tiled room containing a bench, a shower, and a wading pool. I just about peed myself from relief. It was like walking into a sauna room, only without the hard-to-breathe part. It was like a spa.

After a brief tour and orientation, Marshall left me to it. I removed all my clothing and stepped into what amounted to a rather large bathtub filled with salt water. Hit the button to turn off the lights.

As soon as I laid back, the water flooded my ear canals, shutting out the external noises. It was dark. My breathing was loud, my heartbeat softer. I heard the occasional rumble of traffic or machinery. When I swallowed, the sound of my back teeth grinding against one another.

I focused on breathing, telling my muscles to relax.

*In. Out. Let go.*

It was then that I started to understand the purpose of this place: a safe space to let go. Let go of the tension in my muscles, of pent-up emotions, of the illusion of control. Let go of the pressure to be productive, of responsibility. Let go of the need to do anything other than breathe and be.

# Time Without Time

*Kiersi Burkhart*

As I was led into my float room and my host told me how to prepare, gave me tips on how to be comfortable, I smiled and nodded, smiled and nodded – but I harbored a mounting nervousness about what I'd gotten myself into.

Then the door clicked shut, and I was alone.

Once in the water with the light off, lying on my back...I became buoyant, like a piece of driftwood. I knew I was stationary, but as darkness settled, it suddenly felt like I was swirling – the way one does when trying to go to sleep while drunk, pulled around in a vortex.

I don't remember when the swirling stopped. My own breath thrummed in my ears, my heartbeat playing the bass line. Darkness ate up everything, whether my eyes were open or closed – I kept forgetting which was which.

In the absolute dark, shapes began to manifest: light worms and shadows, starbursts and sparks, as if my eyes couldn't believe the true darkness before them and needed to make something up to fill the space.

As the dark stayed, unchanging...I started to panic.

Was this it? Just blackness and silence, just me and myself and

I? How could I possibly bear this much of just me for an entire ninety minutes? Surely I'd be bored of this in ten minutes flat.

I tried to think. I summoned my list of thinking-topics – ones I'd planned in advance – but my mind tsk-tsked at all of them. I couldn't hold onto a single thought for more than a few seconds before my mind moseyed on. Soon, my mind fell silent. It began drifting away from me like a lost balloon.

I stopped trying to hold onto it, and let it go.

Time forgot me, as I forgot time. In the pool, we parted ways; an amicable separation. For a while, we simply didn't need each other. And that was okay.

Thankfully, time is also forgiving. When I was ready, and my float was over, it took me back like a remorseful lover.

# Transmutation

*Courtney Watson*

In a room swallowed by darkness, I sink deeper into my subconscious. Allowing the words to slip away and be replaced by pictured replicas of the soul's journey. Delicate images are birthed and swiftly decay behind my closed eyes. I do not seek after them, I do not require them to stay or ask that they be remembered. I house their existence within, offering space until the space is no longer necessary.

I sit staring out at the cosmos. At the brightly burning sun that washes our earth in life and ask not for an explanation. Feet dangling in dark matter, I recline amongst a bed of stardust. The moon winks playfully as it ducks behind Mother Earth, calling out in its ancient tone that this is a life of exploration. Eyes scanning the expanse, I sink deeper into the feeling. I can see beyond all previously held horizons and I question. What's to come? There are boundaries waiting to be broken still, and ideologies waiting to be challenged. Waves roll over my skin, breath reaches out to be held by something, anything...

Heat. Burning wood that assaults the senses. Crackling embers, shooting docile missiles wherever they feel compelled. I feel the heat rising, nipping at the alcove that houses my sacral. The only way out is through, of course. But how? All conscious energy is placed within, stoking the flames, adding more organics. The heat makes its way up into the ribcage where a caldron is boiling. Boiling the stagnant water that has been sitting for too long, now active and alive with purpose. I can feel the debris begin to separate, the growth begins to die off. Rising from the heat, steam floods my heart and throat and mind. It fogs my inner vision until I am forced to let go of the control I have been so desperately clinging to...

Worlds are still. No words are produced in this moment, possibly all moments hereafter. I am. Draped in light and wonder of all things that be, or have, or will. It is here that I sense my state. Breathing for infinite crevices, scattered among endless timelines. I extend through all. And I am We. And We are here, breathing past the last heartbeat. Breathing through the epochs and extinctions. Breathing into the unknown. For what else is there? Even in the past, We do not know, We cannot tell. So We sit: here, now. Light penetrating through the crown, extending to all higher realms, and down into the plane that houses Us. Fanning out around the masked bed of consciousness with a golden haze. Seeking to be recognized, but content in the understanding of self. The pillar rises, connecting with the seat of all creation. In this moment, We give ourselves over. We have found home.

Home finds its way back through to the conscious mind. Creativity is bursting at the seams, and images without words must be recorded. I find my peace with graphite pencils and worn paper.

# Lightness

*Rooze Garcia*

*Just turn off the light.* Hand on the switch, I hesitate. *You can always turn it back on.* I wonder if I said that out loud? Then I wonder if I wondered that out loud…. *You're avoiding this. Turn off the light. It will be fine.*

A soothing orange glow from the salt lamp makes the otherwise intense darkness bearable. Calming, even. I am breathing still; that's a good sign. I continue breathing and make my way to the tank. *Was there a step? Am I going to stub my toe?* No. No step. I feel the entrance to the capsule, and place the blue swimming noodle into the space the door will lower onto. I step one leg into the salinated water, then the other.

The logistics of this tank are different from the pool room, where the familiarity of the shape and openness created an instant sense of comfort and anticipation. This smaller capsule does not evoke the same sense of expansiveness. I kneel, focus on my breathing, grab the handle on the door and pull it down onto the pool noodle.

In the tiny gap created by that blue piece of pool equipment, the salt lamp's light becomes my safety device. I am 43 years old and afraid of the dark. And now I'm in a small capsule designed to block out light and sound and 90% of gravity's pull. It is not designed to block out my fears. I have to work on that part myself.

~

Time is impossible to track once I'm floating. It's like silly putty: stretching out long one minute then snapping back into a tight ball the next. At the start, I can't stop thinking about work and am wondering if I should schedule my next float to be 2.5 hours instead of 1.5 hours to give me more time to decompress. I'm fantasizing about the luxury of that when my ever-present observer voice chimes in: You are missing this float right now. You are here. I focus on my breath until I forget to and moments later I'm tense and anxious and wondering how I'll get through listening to the sound of my heartbeat for an hour and half. I open my eyes and – for a brief moment – panic; the sliver of light is too far away. I push my feet against the wall of the tank and propel closer to the door.

~

Maybe it was a minute later or 10 minutes or 100 lifetimes. My mind has stopped chasing its own tail and my body has settled into nothing but breath and heartbeat. For now, it is comfortable rather than annoying. I smile a little at the ridiculousness of being annoyed by the sound of one's own heart.

~

The darkness feels darker. I refuse to open my eyes.

~

It's beautiful, the dark tunnel with a dancing stream of blue light. Not a singular light at the end of the proverbial tunnel but a beam of light in motion. White with blue light trails etched against the dark spiral of a tunnel. I try to follow it but the trying makes it disappear.

~

It is time. Not because I hear the music playing, letting me know the session is up, but because some quiet voice has decided it is so. I make my way to the tank door, completely ungracefully manage to get back into a kneeling position, and push against the door. Slide the pool noodle out; then take a slow deliberate breath and pull the door closed. I do not remove my left hand from the door handle. The right one is right in front of my face. I know this because I feel my breath against it. Eyes open, I cannot see a thing.

# Looking for Diamonds in Dirt

*Steven E Parton*

My mind began to sift through my thoughts like one looks for diamonds in dirt. Triviality clung to consciousness, but I lifted the fingers of these superfluous concerns from the edge of my concentration and watched them fall away into nothingness.

At first it was difficult, allowing my mind to relax and grow comfortable with this unusual circumstance. I focused on my breath to empower myself, giving it the attention of balance – breathe in for four seconds, out for four seconds. In... Out...

I told my body there was no reason to be tense here. I asked it to relinquish control of my muscles; for once in their long existence none of them were needed. This took a gentle effort, a timely massaging of will and minor adjustments to my form.

Soon I was left with the core worries that had perpetuated throughout my recent days: where was I going to live in the coming month? Could I count on a steady stream of work in my freelancing? What did the future hold?

In... out...

The tank was pitch black, total imperceptible darkness. But not to me. Even behind closed eyelids, whites and greys danced in my vision, slowly morphing shapes that flowed like liquid dualities until they unwound themselves into dissipating tendrils of third-eye essence.

Eventually my mind simply blanked, like a vast endless horizon with no variance in shape or color. A simple, flat plane of awareness.

There in that darkness, once I had emptied my mind of all my worries of the world, the only thing left was a replay of meaningful relationships. After I passed through those jovial memories with friends, the lasting image that hung in my consciousness was that of the women whom I'd held dearly in bed, their skin pressed against mine, the two of us embracing complete vulnerability as we shared things only true lovers could.

Soon, though, even those images faded, and I became lost in wavelength of thought that was nothing other than pure meditation. And then there was music, a siren's call back to reality. I left my dreamscape with some hesitance and returned to that shared realm we all call reality, feeling freed from many useless stresses and lifted by new appreciations.

# Surface

*C. Starling*

### I.

I can't stop thinking, my thoughts are racing — yesterday, today, tomorrow, work, dinner, family — without a screen to distract me or a task to distract me or the next thing and the next thing, over and over until I fall asleep at night, I can't stop, I don't remember how to stop, I don't want to stop because what happens if I stop, so I keep going and I let my thoughts unfurl and sprint, watch them as they go over everything from yesterday, today, tomorrow for the third, fourth, fifth time.

### II.

I come here to slow down, to breathe, to float, to be light and easy, but it takes a bit to get there, I have to let my brain run its course, it needs to tire itself out like a dog on the beach before she comes home, tired, and sleeps by the fire, I need to let my mind do what it needs to do, I need to accept that it might be fast or might be slow.

### III.

I need to trust that I know exactly what I need, because who else would know what I need – so I take another breath and let my thoughts find their own path, I don't hold them, don't force them, and soon I'm just breathing.

IV.

I sink down into myself even though my body's floating, and this time it feels like a heavy, warm embrace, it feels like I'm being held, it feels like there's nothing left to worry about.

V.

I am where I wanted to be, where I came from.

VI.

I am.

# Out of the Comfort Zone: My Small Tank Experience

*Margot Bigg*

Psychologists and motivational speakers seem to always be jabbering on about the importance facing your fears. Therapists encourage agoraphobic patients to get out and socialize (although usually in a controlled environment) and many a self-help guru lauds the power of stepping out of your comfort zone as a catalyst for personal growth.

However, I've never considered myself a particularly fearful, or even phobic, person. I'm admittedly skittish around the three-inch-long flying cockroaches that live in the tropics, and I'm not super keen on swimming with fish that measure more than an inch long, but I'll gladly look off the edge of tall buildings, and I am happy to share my living space with spiders. Still, if I believed in hell, my personal version would be a room the size of a bathroom stall, with no windows and around-the-clock fluorescent lighting. While I'm not particularly prone to claustrophobia, like many people, I cringe at the idea of being stuck anywhere, much less in a small, enclosed space.

That's why I've always made a point to request spacious, floor-to-ceiling tanks when going for a float. The old-school cocoon-style float tanks reminded me of coffins, and a completely irrational apprehension of feeling stuck inside kept me from ever trying one out.

So I tried one out.

I started my float slowly but surely, with the lid open. The lights were off in the room that held the tank, save for a small salt crystal lamp that served as a nightlight, illuminating the inside of the tank to about the same degree as what you'd get if you left your bedroom curtains open during a full moon. After getting used to being in the space, I decided to close the lid, but would push it open a crack with my foot every couple of minutes, more as a reminder that I could easily get out if need be. Eventually I stopped doing this and allowed myself to drift into float state. When music began to pulse through the water to let me know my 90 minutes was up, I didn't climb out immediately as I always had in the past. I instead savored every last second of my time in the tank. I had never felt more reluctant to get out of a tank, never wished that I could hit some sort of snooze button and stay in for another hour. I had been converted.

For anyone who is apprehensive or even fearful of the smaller tanks, allow me to try to put your mind at ease with what I learned from my small tank float:

1

The smaller isolation tanks are nothing like coffins. They are wide enough to accommodate a broad-shouldered person without fear of bumping the sides, and spacious enough that you can put your arm up perpendicular to your body and still not touch the ceiling. I was able to easily sit up in my tank, with plenty of space to spare, and I imagine that most people shorter than a typical basketball player would be able to, as well.

## 2

It's just as easy to breathe in the smaller isolation tanks as it is in larger float rooms. I can only assume that the tanks are equipped with a sort of stellar ventilation system that allows oxygen to flow in and out without compromising on light or sound isolation.

## 3

Once you get used to them, the smaller isolation tanks are actually less scary than the larger spaces. When I first started floating in larger tanks, I'd often lose my sense of orientation. I'd end up turned around in a different position and come to at a completely different angle than I expected. If you've ever woken in the middle of the night while sleeping in an unfamiliar place, or even just moved your bed to a different part of your room, you've probably experienced something like this, and it can be disconcerting. But in the smaller isolation tanks, there's not enough space to turn around, so you don't risk losing your sense of orientation when you emerge from float state.

## 4

Relinquishing control is essential to the float experience. I think one of my major concerns about being in a small tank was not a standard case of claustrophobia so much as a type-A obsession with being in charge of my surroundings. Most of us like things to be a certain way and get a bit rattled when our environment is not how we like it. Giving up that control and just being was incredibly freeing, and was much easier to do when I didn't have to worry about which way I was faced.

# Existential Enlightenment

*Donovan James*

Existence is an incredible thing – how could we ever forget this? Is it our mass culture of superficiality, our dependence upon drugs of all kinds, whether they're the drink or the pill? Or is it some totality of worldview, spiraling down through the history of our forefathers, leading us further and further from the Tao – the way, the road of a meaningful and grateful life – and closer and closer to our own extinction, both biologically and culturally, as lost and deserted humans drunk on ennui, the doomed children of a blasphemous civilization?

Floating allows us the rare opportunity of a spiritual shower. There are other sources – meditation, yoga, psychedelics. But with floating, there's no opportunity for escape because there's simply nowhere to go. And eventually, all those thoughts that hound you – about your weight, credit card debt, or job – they burn off. They reveal themselves as what they truly are: floating clouds of consciousness that simply pass by.

The aftereffects are similar to those of meditation. The mind is clear – the world seems more vibrant, louder, and there is less space between your thoughts and reality. You are right here. It shears off layers of mental distractions, and brings the distance between your thoughts and reality to zero, which is enlightenment, if a metaphor can capture the meaning of such a word.

As I walked home I was left with a tremendous feeling of gratitude. We are marvelously lucky to even be experiencing this. Think of the millions dead, never born, or the billions that suffer far more than you or I. Think of the infinite stories and moments – either predestined, fated by God, or coincidental – that have come before you. And you are living in the newest moment anyone has ever experienced.

# "A Float Tank's Terms and Conditions"

*Nikki Burian*

There are things in this life that scare you. I am not one of them.
There are things in this life that ruin you. I am not one of them.
Now, I knew what you were initially thinking, anxious poet:
"This will rob me of my sight and my sound,
and I mostly shout these days – far too fragile to
unearth the parts of me that only dwell in harmony.
Just hurt me. Hurt me and I will easily create.
Nurture me, and I do not know how.
I ache for booming, crashing waves,
destructive enough to stifle what cannot clamor."
What I need to tell you, poet, is that I am not upheaval.
I am no exclamation.
I will not drag you through pandemonium
and thunder revelations from you.
I am salt-dissolved buoyancy, cradling your mind above water.
You will not know where I end and where you begin,
I am your warmth. I am comfort disguised as you.
You cannot drown in me in order to be something. I refuse it.
I'm sure I am not the first body you've tried to float in.
I hope I am never the last.

Salt burns open wounds, I don't blame your hesitation.

But remember, I am a carrier.

I will bring you, silent and confident, to the person you want to be.

If you agree to these terms and conditions, sign below:

# When Things Are Quiet

*K.C. Swain*

The silence of floating is what gets me.

I have always been at odds with the static in my head and the friction of human life. Normal life distractions lose their physical weight and become nothing as they float from my space in the tank. The silence is another slice of me that I forgot about.

That slice of me that is put away by life.

Silence is its own character we forget about unless we are forced to face it. It's my ally. It's me and it's always awkward meeting yourself again after a short hiatus. The silence makes me realize how long I've been gone, but reminds me that I'm home again and don't need to worry.

The physical form takes a break, but my mind is free – free to float around my problems, solutions, past, present, and future. Maybe this is me, seeing in four dimensions like the aliens in Slaughterhouse Five.

It always feels like I'm plugging back into myself, but also into the void. The universe. The muse goddess. The arts. The beats and rhythms. The love. It's like a time warp. As though I've slept a week while the outside world rolls on at the same speed. It's nice when you realize you can step away.

I know the full body relaxation is beginning when I feel the vertebrae in my neck and back let go. Being in the float state for this makes the experience extremely eerie in the best way. I can feel and visualize the tissues letting go. Stress is trying to escape from my body, and what a show it is. With each pop in my neck and back, there is a corresponding release in my face, legs, hands, feet, and core. My face tingles with joy. At this point I fully let go and let my body upgrade.

The pops are loud. Sometimes they echo from faraway places in my body. Must be stress literally screaming out of my body. I love it: this is when I know the forces of the float are truly taking hold. I knew these things would happen. On my first float, my float guide told the three of us newbies that our bodies, once they relaxed, would start getting loud. Loud like that asshole we all hate in a crowded room. He said it was nothing to be scared of. This is the body and mind shaking off the rust holding us back.

# Packing for the Voyage

*Ken Yoshikawa*


I am at an utter loss for words
except the ones that fit my belt loop.
But I'm naked, and I don't know where I am
or rather, where I came from.
I remember packing for the voyage:
washing my face, drawing circles round my feet,
strapping my pen to my earlobe
& my notes to my eyelid insides.
Saying: I'm going somewhere special
to mount pyramids on my head
and gaze down monsters in the pastureland:
to light them down right to the nails.
I'm bound out to chain a galaxy,
bring it home and hook it to my windowsill.
However, pushing out into the tide
that cozy beach becomes a coin-edge,
becomes a locket full of past that sinks away.
I've lost my grip while sailing on a mote of dust.
I dare not say a thing.
It's times like these,
when the monsters I set out to slay

come out, to hang from my eyelashes,
and start to bite a way through all my hard work;
when I can't help but walk lost into the bloody room inside my head;
it's times like these that something,
not unlike Gandalf the Grey
gruff and hushed
comes to, speaks up, and tells me:

When harbor's at a loss,
for being stranded at the stand still,
it's okay to be afraid. Please mind the current.
Greet uncertainty with "Hey,"
and watch your throat catch fire.
It isn't time for you to drown.
I am still here.

Illustration by Levi Greenacres

# Eons

*Rooze Garcia*

At first I stretch out, play
against buoyant salt-saturated water
a viscosity somewhere between the Gulf
and ballistic gel (I do not know who shot
J.R. or the deputy but someone confessed
to the sheriff's demise). A debris field
of thoughts breaks through the tension
surfaces and my body forms an X – da Vinci's
man becomes woman becomes weightless
I go through the motions each one from X
to a long I and back to nothing but this
beat thump beat thump thump beat and breathe
in and out, concentrate a diaphragmatic breath
focus, out a long exhale of atoms, in
my stomach swells and suddenly I am afraid:
I did not lock the door. Eyes open and lights
bring me back into the room. I orient, off-center
in the squared pool. On the door, there is a sign:
Float in Progress. Who would cause a disturbance
in such a place? I close my eyes and promise
next time I'll lock the door; this time

I want to stay in this diaphanous net, cradled
against gravity, against decades of cultural
chatter flooding my brain (did you know:
stars in the sky outnumber grains of sand
on earth, and yet one grain, just one tiny grain
holds more atoms than there are stars
in the universe?) How long do I float
before my mind slips into the space
between stars, before the subtle shift in water
becomes the rocking of tiny waves pulsing out
from the rhythmic constancy of my own heart?

# Embodiment

*Sione Aeschliman*

This time, none of the hypersensitivity. Instead I begin to meditate on place, on where I've been recently.

A vision of myself at a bar with a friend for a show and what it felt like to be there. Like I was standing beside myself.

I think I've spent most of my life standing beside myself rather than being fully in my body and fully present in the moment. But why?

Because it hasn't felt safe.

One of my friends talks about having abandoned herself; maybe this is what she means. I too abandoned myself at a young age. Somehow decided that it wasn't safe to be in my own body.

\* \* \*

I drift. The sensation of layers of myself being peeled off. But it doesn't hurt. It isn't even uncomfortable. Each layer of myself is a thin, fuzzy blanket that, when pulled back, reveals another thin layer of fuzzy blanket. Each layer peeled back leaves me more vulnerable but still safe. Four layers in and I'm still not at the bottom.

I am my own fuzzy blanket, I realize.

I am my own safe space.

It was never something I needed to find or create for myself; it always existed within . I am it.

* * *

It's hard to let go of the tension in my body. Sometimes it feels like the only thing holding me together. Without it, I might fly apart and lose my sense of self.

* * *

Before entering this float, I set an intention to further deepen my connection with myself and to understand more about my spiritual journey. I have my answer: I want to figure out how to step back into my body and stay there in the uncomfortable moments. To cease abandoning myself. To stop trying to control everything and instead recognize that I am always, and have always been, safe.

* * *

"Your eyes are so bright!" my friend said when I entered the lobby after my float.

"Are my pupils huge?" I asked, wondering if I looked drugged-out like I did after my last float.

"No, they're just really bright. You look happy."

And the next day I felt it: I found myself singing and humming, dancing along to the music I'd put on. For the first time in a long time, relaxed and secure enough to be playful.

# Float

*Tasha Jamison*

busyness and nervous energy and the weight of expectation and the chorus of voices in your head that comes from rehearsing conversation after conversation and performance after performance and the way it all dissolves in water like so many mineral obligations and it all comes out neutral and slick and warm and it all wraps you up in safety and comfort but you can't quite stretch out far enough but you can't quite forget that you are enclosed even as you lose track of where you are in space even as you lose track of where you are in time and the familiar voices are still there but they can go on without you they don't need you to play host this time they can solve their own problems so just sit back and experience your own company so just witness the way each part plays off another just soak it in soak in the sting and the buoyancy and the bitterness and the joy and don't be afraid to let go and don't be afraid to play and don't be afraid to fall asleep because this time there will be someone to tuck you in because this time there will be someone to turn out the lights and they will step out so softly that they won't wake you and you can rest and in the morning you can remember what it was to trust another person and in the morning you can remember what it was to trust yourself

# A Guide to Floating for the Anxious Mind

*C. Starling*

Breathe in. One.

Breathe out. Two.

Keep the count going. Three.

At first you're going to be afraid. That's normal, for you. You're afraid a lot, more than you realize. But here, in the dark, in the quiet, you're going to realize it – loudly, brightly, overwhelmingly.

You are afraid.

You are also safe.

You've forgotten how to accept safety.

Breathe in.

Breathe out.

You sit up. You turn the light on. You regret it immediately; the relief seems hollow, because now that the light is on, you know you were always safe.

Turn the light off.

Lie back down.

What was the count?

Breathe in. One.

Breathe out. Two.

Fear nibbles at your heart.

Breathe out. Four.

But maybe, you think, you can just let it, and it will get bored. It will go away.

This time, the fear isn't immediate. It isn't as sharp-edged and gleaming. It creeps along your skin, in tiny crawling steps. You tense. You close your eyes.

You reach for the side of the tank.

You find the light.

You try to breathe through the fear, but in a moment of weakness, you turn the light back on. The water sloshes around you. The world is upended for just a moment.

And you are alone in the tank.

You are safe.

You hate yourself for these tricks your mind plays on you. You feel weak. You feel angry.

You turn the light back off.

Breathe in. One.

Breathe out. Two.

A pang of shame – are you doing this all wrong? Isn't this supposed to feel transcendent?

Are you wasting your time?

Money?

Will you ever be able to relax enough to do this right?

Breathe in. Seven.

You need to trust yourself.

You need to stop over-analyzing.

You need to just be.

Breathe in. One.

There is you, in the dark, and there's nothing you can look at. Nothing you need to look at. No responsibility to look, always look, *always keep yourself safe, you never know when something could hurt you, always be on alert even when there's nothing to be afraid of.*

Nobody needs anything from you right now.

Breath out. Four.

The realization settles into you, and before you know it

You

Are

Boundless

Breathe in. Nine.

You feel the water shift gently against your skin, and you smile.

There is wonder in your chest.

There is curiosity in your breath as you breathe out. Two.

The darkness no longer scares you. Nothing is in the darkness here. You are the dark. The endless expanse. No boundaries in sight, nothing stalking you.

Remove the outside world, and you are free to be yourself.

To be the you that you locked away years ago, when you learned the world was a scary place.

To be the you that you'd forgotten about.

You feel it glowing in the core of you, a round polished pulsing stone of childlike wonder. You feel your kindness, your happiness, your generosity. You've always known they were in there, somewhere, but now you feel it.

You've lost the count, but it doesn't matter now.

Breathe in, one. You can come back to this anytime you need it.

Breathe out, two. You can drift now, and explore memories and thoughts and feelings you haven't let yourself touch in years.

Breathe in, three. You are boundless, floating in the expanse, spreading out to your full self.

You hadn't realized you were curled up so tightly.

You hadn't realized you'd made yourself so much smaller.

You've missed you.

You are home.

The music starts slowly, distantly, and you emerge from the expanse on legs like a newborn foal, shaky and excited and bright.

The sunlight outside is bliss.

The walk to the bus is a revelation.

And no matter how far the bus takes you from that expanse, all you need to return is:

Breathe in. One.

Breathe out. Two.

The count will bring you home.

# The In-between

*K.C. Swain*

The visuals start within the first few moments of the float. Usually they don't come until later. It's like a switch flipped when my head hits the water. My body pops up, and instantly the flow state begins. I close my eyes and go down the rabbit hole. Visible static comes from the corner of my eyes and then morphs into a swirling light show: a liquid checkerboard folding in and out of itself. Then it switches gears and spins in the opposite direction. A hypnosis wheel to my daydreams. I get this idea that floating may be the in-between place that sits in the middle of being awake and sleeping.

I realize I haven't been letting go of things. Ideas about why I haven't been expressing myself begin coming into focus. I need to make more music and share it. Not because I'm good, because it makes me happy. All these ideas need to go somewhere or they swim in my head 'til I find them important. They rattle in my head at around five a.m. every day and later in the evening when I'm beat, tired, and bent. They make me want to move. In my float state I realize they are just thoughts. I can get rid of them when I want – on paper or through chatting – but the big downer is when I don't.

Holding things in creates more work than letting go. It seems silly that my mind won't let go but my neck and back will, no problem. Things are simpler when I float; I find myself able to separate myself from myself. I can breathe life into my decisions and dance with my thoughts like they're leaving. Floating lubes the situation and guides me to the realization that I have the power to let go and express the stress in me. It doesn't have to sit inside.

# Meditations on Meditating

*Tanya Jarvik*

My husband's aunt used to meditate for two hours every day: one hour at dawn, and one hour at dusk. She had to keep track of when the sun came up and went down, so that she could be sure to begin meditating at just the right moment. Whenever she visited, we had to plan around her schedule, which was a pain, especially in the winter, when her sessions interfered with both breakfast and dinner.

Barbara claimed that following this strict meditation practice had saved her life. Maybe she was right about that, because by all accounts, she had been a miserably self-absorbed teenager, a Jewish-American Princess whose initial interest in Eastern philosophy and asceticism seemed to have been fueled by a desperate desire to say some kind of big "fuck you" to her doting but clueless parents. She joined a commune as a young adult, and didn't have much interaction with anyone in her family for many years.

When I first met Barbara, she was only about fifty, but she already carried herself like an old lady. Although she had recently left her commune – for reasons she wouldn't divulge, although we later learned some unsavory things about the man who billed himself as its spiritual leader – she still gazed at a picture of her guru whenever she meditated. I liked Barbara, but she struck me as definitely strange. Meditating, therefore, also seemed strange to me, since I didn't know anyone else who did it.

My opinion of meditation did not improve over the next decade, either, as I watched Aunt Barbara rejoin the world. She got certified as an elementary school teacher, bought a house and a car, began wearing jeans and tank tops, and cut her hair. As her life got busier, she also became much more lax about her meditation practice – first paring down the sessions to forty-five minutes or half an hour, then occasionally skipping the evening sit, then just doing a morning sit, and finally giving up on her practice altogether. She still meditated – sometimes. When it suited her. And she seemed like a much happier person.

Barbara's life story reminds me of the plotline of a book I read in high school: Hermann Hesse's Siddhartha. The main character was born into a life of ease, which he leaves. He spends decades perfecting the art of meditation, pouring all of his energy into achieving spiritual mastery, but ultimately he's not satisfied with his life as a monk. Disillusioned, he takes up residence in a village and throws himself into building wealth and prestige. At the pinnacle of his power, he falls in love with a prostitute. He becomes so enamored with her that he loses interest in everything else, and as a result, he loses his fortune. Since the prostitute is only interested in his money, she leaves him. However, she's pregnant with his child by this point, and somehow Siddhartha ends up caring for this boy – who grows up to be a most ungrateful little bastard. It's only then, selflessly serving his son with no expectation of reward or even gratitude, that Siddhartha reaches a state of true wisdom.

I have no idea what message Hesse intended his book to

convey, but the message I took from it, as a callow teenager required to read at least one German "classic" if I wanted to pass Frau Schmidt's class, was that meditation was a selfish waste of time. Watching Barbara's transformation a few years later, that message was reiterated and reinforced. There was no way I was ever going to take up meditation. I did dabble a bit in yoga in my twenties, which meant participating in the occasional guided meditation at the end of class: all of us on our backs, on ragtag mats at the JCC, lights out, eyes dutifully closed while the peppy septuagenarian instructor reminded us to relax, to focus on our breathing. But that hardly counted.

In my thirties, in the midst of a bad breakup with a friend, completely at a loss, I read Pema Chödrön's When Things Fall Apart: Heart Advice for Difficult Times, and I began to think, for the first time, that meditation might be a good thing to try sometime. However, I didn't actually do anything with this particular thought, this slight shift in stance. I merely went on living my life – which, by the time I turned forty, did happen to include several practices one might describe as meditative. Still, although I was running, and knitting, and writing on a regular basis, and although these activities clearly helped me to center myself, I persisted in thinking of myself as someone who just did not meditate.

And then yesterday, alone in the dark of a sensory deprivation tank, buoyed up by warm water so loaded with Epsom salts that I was able to relax every muscle in my body, I experienced a moment – or several moments? – in which I did not have a single thought. My mind was blank. Of course, the second I realized that I hadn't noticed an idea or an image or a sensation cross my mind in... however long it had been, I immediately started thinking again.

I thought about people, mostly. People I live with, people I love, people I used to love, people who played their bit parts in the performance of my life and then exited the stage, people who died long ago in wars I've only read about, people who exist only in books, and people I only imagine exist, somewhere else on this planet, doing whatever it is they do: riding in taxis and subways, hustling to work or curling up on the couch at home, holding out copper alms bowls, putting on elaborately embroidered slippers, staring at computer screens in tiny cubicles, tending lovingly to their horses or beating their children, reroofing their houses with slate or straw or asphalt shingles or palm fronds, eating or sleeping or fucking...in short, being human.

The idea that occurred to me yesterday, after noticing that I had inadvertently managed to clear my mind for a moment, goes something like this: if we are not singular creatures, if in fact we are all connected, then meditation cannot be a selfish act. Each thing one person does, or fails to do, is done by us all together.

# The Stars Cracked My Face Open

*Dot Hearn*

My body dropped into sync with the water almost immediately. Maybe because this was the first time I'd had two floats so close together; or not. That relieving sensation of not knowing where my physical body ends or begins in relation to the water. Of being one with the salt-infused water. . .or is it the water-infused salt? Which comes first: salt / water? Question faded with the realization that it's all the same.

I'd left the tank's stars on overhead for a minute. Maybe two. Stars rippled like the water: dimmed and brightened and faded, wandering through the white to blue spectrum and back. Beautiful. Pretty to look at but they kept my body anchored to my location in space, so I bid them goodnight and welcomed the complete darkness. I let my body drift into the void of salt / water / skin. Heart beat.

With my body lost to the salt / water, distractions of mind drifted away faster, easier. Thoughts about work that day, emails not yet returned, a date of service I forgot on an invoice, factors to consider about a workshop in October and. Stop. The list of what I coulda / shoulda / woulda done stopped. As my body bobbed with my heartbeat / breath making small outward ripples from me to the edges of the tank.

My body drifted, as it does, and occasionally a finger touched an edge. A toe. The other foot. A hand. Then I floated suspended in darkness with thoughts quiet and breathing slowed. Listening to my body rhythms and watching darkness pulse. Nearly shapeless. A sparkle off to the left of what would be my peripheral vision in light, which faded out as fast as it had appeared.

Then sounds. A low hum like a table. Like one of the droning loops from my pink Buddha Machine. I listened to the music and wondered if it was real from outside of my body or if it lived only in my mind. I knew it wasn't time to get out; my float had just begun.

I raised my head until my ears were out of the water and listened. Silence. There was a faint rumble of a bus passing on the street outside, but otherwise. Nothing. I lowered my head, returned ears into, the familiar air bubbles rising to seal out water. Quiet.

The return of the quiet, meditative rumble.

Floating. Listening to my body music, more ear bubbles popping. Watching a parade of darkness. No expectations except to be present. Floating. A tear from my right eye ran down toward the water, I thought. I let it go and wondered if it was a tear, or memory of a tear, without a cause.

I reminded myself to not touch with my saltwater-soaked hands as I felt pricks randomly cover my face; like holding lit sparklers as a kid on the Fourth of July. Remembering the sparks jumping from the lit end of the sizzling stick onto my hands and they didn't hurt, but I could feel them. It was like that, and my mind explained that the stars had cracked my face open with star-sparks and I felt tiny fissures explode across my face. Then smiling crackles erupted on the parts of my arms immersed in water. On one ankle.

I blinked. I think. I listened for the now-absent beating sound. Nothing. Blinked again and it was still dark. Felt nothing but the water floating body salt edges on my skin.

And again. The stars reached out and touched my face but now I knew I would be fine. I floated and noticed. Noticed there were no more tears and wondered how long I'd been floating how much more time was left. Closed my eyes noticed breathing heart beating. Silent stillness.

# Gravity

*Margot Bigg*

Gravity – much like oxygen – is something most of us take for granted, or at least those of us who aren't astronauts. This invisible, omnipresent force keeps us firmly rooted on Planet Earth, and though we don't actually feel it, it's always there, pulling us down just enough to keep us from floating off into the sky, but not so much that it crushes us into the soil.

When I was eight or nine years old, I read an article about astronauts preparing for stints in space in special anti-gravity chambers, and I was determined to get in on the action. I figured that by the time I was old enough to travel to NASA, anti-gravity chambers would be popular and open to the public at science museums and theme parks.

But then I grew up and forgot that a tumble around an anti-gravity chamber was on my childhood bucket list. Still, every once in a while, I would hear, see, or experience something that would remind me of how much I wanted to experience the absence of gravity at least once in my life.

The first trigger was also the most obvious: an acquaintance had participated in an experiment at NASA's Zero-Gravity Research Center and had the photos to prove it, which she naturally posted on Facebook by the dozen.

Then there was the time that I tried indoor skydiving at an enormous indoor adventure center that also had a wave pool for surfing and an indoor ski slope. I was suited up, taught the correct skydiving positioning, and brought to the inside of an oval wind tunnel that had been fitted out with fans to simulate the sensation of flying. Under the guidance of an instructor who had left his job as a gymnast at a traveling circus to teach people the art of indoor skydiving, I was able to float up and down the tunnel, angling the arch in my back and the position of my arms to increase and decrease the resistance between my body and the air circulating in the tunnel. But I wasn't defying gravity. It was gravity that made the resistance that allowed me to "fly" possible.

And along came floating. I'd heard that the sensation of floating in an isolation tank was the closest one could get to experiencing the anti-gravity effect without either becoming an astronaut or paying hundreds or maybe thousands of dollars for a ride in a zero-gravity flight on an airplane. So I tried it.

Initially, I couldn't stop thinking about the fact that I was floating, feeling the slick saltiness on my skin, wondering how long it would take before the lines between my body and the water would start to fade away. My mind was chattering away, as it usually does throughout my waking hours, making mental grocery lists, wondering what my friends were up to at that very moment, and remembering the things I had to get done, all set to a soundtrack of whatever catchy song happened to be stuck in my head.

But as I floated, the din of this internal prattle began to fade, and soon I was left only with the steady thump of my heartbeat. This constant pounding was the only thing keeping me tethered to my body. I could no longer feel the water that was keeping me afloat, could no longer distinguish where "I" stopped and "it" started. And at that very moment gravity – or its absence – no longer mattered.

# Run

*Ken Yoshikawa*


I've always hated being cold.
[RUN PROGRAM. . . . . . . .(SYSTEM_DIAGNOSTIC)]

Rebuilding blanket cradles for myself, I'm determined to out-
snooze the hermit crab.
[DIAGRAM . . . . . . . . . . (MENTAL_IMAGES);
CORRELATE . . . . . . . . . (EMOTIONAL_CONTEXT);
IDENTIFY TRAJECTORY . . . (PAST, FUTURE, PRESENT);
IMPLEMENT . . . . . . . . . (COURSE_RELAY_HOMEOSTASIS)]

I can plan a whole day with my head under the covers.
[INITIATE? Y/N]

I will come to an end one day, so why bother?
[TRAJECTORY ACQUIRED: FUTURE, DISREGARD INQUIRY]

Where did I come from that I cannot burrow back?
[TRAJECTORY ACQUIRED, PAST: DISREGARD INQUIRY]

This will end like a loaded spring frozen in a cube.
It will melt and shatter out from the inside.

Am I that endless spiral when it rolls on down the staircase? I just can't tell.
[TRAJECTORY ACQUIRED: PRESENT, ACCEPT CORRESPONDENCE]

There is a face of an old torment dipping down and watching from the ceiling.
Great, my own haunting: Ol' Empty Eyes.
[POTENTIAL MALWARE DETECTED, ANALYZING...]

Crack it like a code. Can't break an echo. Can only watch it dance until it stops.
[REMOVE THREAT? Y/N]

The dark behind the ghost is deeper, clean and innocent.
I remember how you made your way inside my head.
[TRAJECTORY ACQUIRED: PAST ATTACHMENT, PRESENT PAIN; REGRET, SHAME, GRIEF ADAPTIVE PROCESS APPLICABLE; DISREGARD PROJECTION]

You yoked me and ripped me.
[DISREGARD PROJECTION]

Brought the ceiling down with the door-lock clack.
[DISREGARD PROJECTION]

You could be right outside this room and find me here right now.
[PRESENT REALITY ASSURES SECURITY; DISREGARD PROJECTION]

I'm fragile. I'm scared against the night. Please keep me warm.

[PRESENT NEED IDENTIFIED, PROCEED WITH CARE]

Gone as quietly as it came.
[THREAT QUARANTINED; CONTINUE DIAGNOSTIC]


Sometimes I shake like I stuck my fingers in the sockets.
[RUN]


Sometimes I decompress the voices from my neck right out my
fingertips.
[RUN]


Sometimes I just let go and find I'm there to catch me.
[RUN]


The heartbeat is a master class,
[SIGNAL DETECTED]


and even running late, I'm right on time.
[DOWNLOADING...]


This week I dreamt an old dead friend & I went surfing.
I've never surfed before.
It was cloudy and the waves were rough.
From a nearby cliff I watched myself bicker on the shore sand.
I dared not be uncomfortable, made cold by ocean water:
all those classic unknown dreads from dipping into chaos.
But something uncurled.
From all those mornings growing up behind my bundle forts &

staying

just one minute longer

in the shower, I braved the chill for the thrill.

That mountain climbers on the tall peaks venture weeks,

that joggers bolt out the door in the morning,

that jumpers fly from open airplane hatches:

I understand.

Now, looking as far as I can

everything is clear.

All I see are stars.

[TRAJECTORY ACQUIRED: PRESENT.

ACCEPT CORRESPONDENCE]

# Unplug and Lift Off

*Steven E Parton*

My consciousness was in desperate need of an unplug. I'd just gotten back from Tokyo, where my mind had been dwarfed by looming vistas of neon lights and assaulted by the echoing cacophony of pachinko parlors, motorcycles, car horns and the accumulated commotion of 35 million mobile residents who make mastering your own spatial awareness a priority at all times.

The float tank shone like a beacon of salvation to this road-weary, over-saturated mind.

I climbed in and drank in the fizzy lifting drink of solace and solitude. There were no white-gloved subway workers here, no Tokyoites whose job was to pack me into commuter trains like one compacts garbage so more rubbish can fit. This vessel was single-occupancy, and like the shape of my floating ship suggested, we were going to the dark and starry void.

As I adjusted to the weightless flight toward the cosmos, I felt my consciousness begin its slow release from my body. I felt like I was sliding away, drifting along some unseen flow through a wormhole of subconscious thoughts. At first I was assaulted, much like I was back in Tokyo, where sensory overload was commonplace. But the further I traversed, the less and less I had to contemplate. The tunnel grew fainter, quieter, the pressure of overwhelming ego subsiding until...

Poof.

Empty space.

The gentle beat of my heart.

The even flow of easy breaths.

There I swam, free of gravity and stimulation and information. A subtle battle between awareness and nothingness was the only action taking place in this realm. And there I stayed, timelessly appreciating the cathartic dance...

...until notes of music told me the spaceship was returning to Earth.

# You Have to Spend Time to Make Time

*Sarah Gallegos*

I always know what to expect. After taking a few floats I feel rather seasoned. Floating takes time. Time away from stress, work, home – time I don't have. I try to reason in my mind how I could possibly carve out a chunk of time to literally lie around and do nothing. Every controlling muscle in my body screams out that there is no way to neglect my responsibilities. In order to balance the scales I negotiate with myself that I will allow myself the time to contemplate and write. I tell myself writing is one of my responsibilities and somehow negotiate the time cost.

While I am lying there – feeling guilty for not getting anything done – my mind wanders and I think about spring, and plants, and bees. I contemplate the health of soils; I look forward to the stone fruits of summer that spring forth from the blooms outside today. I visualize blossoms flowing in the breeze. The sound of cicadas at night hum in my mind.

Then it hits me. I can never expect my own fruit to be ripe and nourish those around me if I don't tend my own soil. If my base system can't feed all the roots attached to me, we will all wither.

The guilt of giving myself a reprieve melts away. In our

endless carrot-chasing endeavors we never really stop and just be. It feels counter-productive and a waste of time. It holds no value for us, yet we pay for it. Timeshares, massages, movie tickets – all just brain vacations. When we spend money just to take 90 minutes away from life, we aren't really helping our wellness. We check out of our minds and welcome in negative stimuli as a way to recharge. We will always be comparing ourselves to everyone else's treasures, constantly seeking more for our own troves.

If I need to feel guilty for doing nothing, it may as well be constructive nothing.

Floating is so passive. But it is also an exercise in presence. Your brain starts checking in on itself. Healing wounds both mental and physical. It is a push and pull between rest and rebirth, stillness and turmoil. You don't expose new hurts by feeling like you don't have as much as those around you – you're alone. There is no one to judge your yoga pose, but also no one to direct you. You have to trust that your body knows what to do – it does.

Today I learned something new. By allowing myself to meditate I am able to be at my best. The guilt I felt was because I thought of floating as checking out, but it is checking in. You become more in tune and attached, more able to face the day. Every minute then becomes more productive and positive, and goes more in the direction I plan for.

You get the time you never want to give yourself to really recover from life. Every trip to the tank is just like life. You plan, make appointments, prepare for your endeavors, and think you know how it will go. But in life things rarely go according to plan. Sometimes you just can't relax, and it goes nowhere. Sometimes you learn to just be, absorb the life around you, and be present.

# It's Just You and What You Brought in With You

*Sione Aeschliman*

"I told you not to get salt water in your eyes," he huffed. The only sign of impatience I'd ever seen from him.

"Yeah, but when you wake up from a nightmare, flailing, and don't know where you are, it's kind of hard to control that kind of thing."

He grunted.

"Lemme ask you something," I said. "When the saltwater dries on you in there, does it…kind of burn?"

He looked thoughtful for a minute. "Not really. I mean it itches, but – "

"No, this burned."

We were silent for a moment. He studied me with something like suspicion.

"It's probably just psychosomatic," I said finally.

"Well I guess," he began, "it could be that in the bigger room it's warmer in there and the salt dries more completely?"

"Yeah, that's okay," I said. "You don't have to try to make me feel better."

"Did it hurt?"

I shook my head. "It was definitely uncomfortable."

"Aw," he said, his tone turning suddenly conciliatory. "I'm sorry that happened."

I was puzzled by his apology. "It's all right," I said. "It's an experience. It was interesting."

"That's a good attitude. I like that."

What other attitude was there? As I considered his response, it occurred to me that some people might come in here having the expectation that this was going to be an entirely comfortable and relaxing experience. That a small percentage of them might complain if they were foolish enough to get salt water in their eyes or they could feel anything physical at all, even if what they felt was all in their heads.

But it wasn't like that for me. I hadn't come in with any expectation that floating in a sensory deprivation tank would be a comfortable experience. I'm afraid of enclosed spaces and of drowning; if I were looking for comfortable, I wouldn't have chosen to do this at all. I chose to do it because I like to challenge myself from time to time by facing things that scare the shit out of me. Such as my imagination.

I'm really good at nightmares. I'm good at thinking of frightening possibilities. I'm good at making myself believe they're real enough to freak out about. I'm good at turning on the light in my sleep, and when my sleep-self can't find the light, I'm good at misinterpreting piles of clothes and curtains as people or creatures with mal intent and waking myself up in a panic.

The last time I'd floated, my mind had constructed images of another person sneaking around the edge of the pool toward me, eels swimming in the water, a spider crouched on my sternum. "The only things here are you and what you brought in with you," I kept repeating. Granted, I could've brought a spider in with me, but highly unlikely that it could've survived the pre-float shower and getting into the tank.

This time, I'd fallen asleep pretty early on and awoken only when I had a nightmare that someone jumped on me. Which is when I sat up, flailing, and had gotten salt water in my eyes.

It was only when I didn't panic, when I realized my reason for wanting to turn on the light wasn't to reassure myself that I was in fact alone in the room but rather so that I could find my towel and wipe the salt water off my face, when I wasn't afraid of this dark – that I realized how afraid of the dark I usually am.

After I turned off the light and laid down again, I became aware of a burning sensation on my right forearm, as if someone had grabbed me roughly. Then on my torso. This is what I would ask about later, even though I already suspected it was in my head. There'd been no burning sensation at the beginning of the float, though water must've been drying on me then, too.

I began to feel antsy. Wondered how long I'd been in the tank and wished that the music would just come on already so I could leave.

If you want to go, just go. You don't have to wait for the music, I reminded myself. It's your choice. Either commit to staying or commit to leaving.

I stayed. I surrendered.

# Stuck In Time

*K.C. Swain*

I have this monumental feeling of being stuck in time physically, but mentally free. When I relax completely, I feel like I am stuck in jello. My mind is trying to understand how I can feel so still in liquid. Is this really water? My understanding of liquid and solid has changed in all the best ways. Losing track of where I begin and end is part of the feeling. I enjoy when this happens in the float sequence. It's interesting to me how the tank with the lights on feels so unfamiliar once I am in the dark. Maybe this is the middle ground between sleeping and waking. I feel it more with my mind than with my body.

My physical form can only go so far, but my mental energy and presence transcends. This is the point when I can reorganize myself into different parts. I couldn't do this without the float experience. A silent question begins to swirl in my head. Is this some form of time travel? Maybe we are thinking of time travel in the wrong context. Maybe time travel is simpler than we realize. Do we need to create some fabulous machine or do we already have the all the tools deep in our minds, and the game is to figure out how to unlock it? Each time I float I feel I'm going somewhere else. Each time builds on the next. Each experience takes me deeper and closer to new answers and better questions. Could I communicate with other floaters? Or something else?

I am a liquid time capsule to my dreams and reality. I feel like Professor Dumbledore swimming in dreams and looking for answers. It's a weird feeling to be sitting above oneself and extracting thoughts like a surgeon. I can see the trouble with physical forms, once I'm able to separate from my own. I also realize I need practice, because I find myself getting freaked out when my ego realizes what I'm doing. This compares to lucid dreaming, when we realize we are dreaming and how the awareness throws us from the altered state. Waking myself up in those moments is fear trying to control the situation. I like the challenge to let that go.

After the float, everything is more vibrant. There is a fabulous glow to everything; call it Hollywood lighting. Light and air seem more magical than ever. I'm reborn when I come out of the tank. I am lighter and clearer. Sharp like a knife when it comes to connected thoughts and what really matters. Letting go is the best medicine. The float experience makes that situation more fluid. Makes me believe I can let go. Shaking off distractions seems like part of the plan and not a mountain to climb. The little things slip away without effort. Big problems lose the "big" and simply become "problems" like the rest, waiting patiently to be worked out. The smile on my face is hard to shake. I am a little beacon of hope walking around post-float. Call me Little Spark Plug! I feel powerful and realize the power I have in this world. I go into the tank a busted-up tuning fork. After 90 minutes of freedom I come out a bright and balanced tuning fork. In tune with the heartbeat of life and the earth. Music sounds different. Songs I have listened to endlessly have a different tune, an added little sound that excites my soul. Everything is new if I let it be.

# Offerings

*Kiersi Burkhart*

I could feel each individual droplet of water as it ran out of the showerhead onto my salty hair, down the sides of my face. A faint buzzing lingered behind my ears, but it faded into the hiss of hot water. I imagine showers rarely sound so loud as when you've just stepped out of a sensory deprivation tank – it's like an icicle falling on a silent, snowy night: a bright clattering, a point of light in total darkness.

That was when I realized I'd been staring at my feet under the water for ten minutes.

Thoughts had to force their way back in, raking their hands through the thin membrane that had formed around my brain inside the tank. I started remembering all the tiny epiphanies I'd had in the darkness, each flitting moment of clarity as it landed on me and, spinning like a perfect, tiny whirligig, blew away all the extraneous matter.

At the host's suggestion, I tried a different float option this time. Last time, I'd floated in the unintimidating open pool that recalled the one I'd grown up swimming in on Saturdays. Today's float would be more old-school – in the "tank." It was a gray box with a small door on the top that swung open like a hatch. Romantic, I thought, as I slid into it feet-first, and my butt slipped on the salty floor. I skidded around a bit before I could grab the handle and pull the tank door closed.

Light along the edges of the rubber seal winked out, and that increasingly familiar absentness settled around me. Inside, the air wasn't much different from the open pool – but it stuck closer to me, and warmer, like a frightened pet cat.

I didn't panic now that I knew a little better what to expect in isolation. I puzzled over why boredom had frightened me so much my first time, and why it didn't now.

I suppose that life had gone on spin cycle; now it was an uncontrolled, chaotic mess. These few protected moments inside the tank? They were mine – every last dark, silent one. As more of them ticked by, my self-satisfaction grew.

The thin, protective membrane, like a spider web, began to form around my brain. Insulating me. Protecting me.

In the close embrace of the tank, holding onto individual ideas and particular thoughts became easy. I stacked them and knocked them over like a child's blocks. I turned them over, squinted at them, organized them by color and shape and size.

And then, they started moving on their own.

Unlike my first float, this time I watched myself disconnecting, like an astronaut as their last cord detaches from the space shuttle.

Still, no panic; just relief. Each thought, each block, each pile of problems – the boy I love, the books waiting to be written, the people wanting things from me, the people I want to give things to, the bill I still haven't paid and the dishes in my sink and the light bulb waiting to be changed – they all lined up, silent and organized, like funeral-goers waiting to peer into a casket.

But the casket was a giant metal dumpster.

One by one they approached the dumpster, and one by one, they dumped in an offering. First, a worry. Then, a concern. More and more blocks of shit, troubles, needling thoughts and squealing fears, thrown onto the pile of garbage.

Once all my attendees were done and neatly lined up on the other side, I tossed in the match.

I floated away from the shuttle untethered, unconcerned, as it all burned. Its white shape faded and faded until it was no more than another star dotting my infinite landscape.

I was still staring at my feet, under the shower stream, when someone knocked on the door.

"Did you hear the music?"

Words?

What were those again?

My head snapped up, and I had to blink a few times before I could answer.

"Yes!" I called. "Yes, I did. Sorry. I'm just taking a long shower."

"No problem," he answered, and footsteps padded down the hall.

I took a long, deep breath, and stepped out of the shower.

Illustration by Mike Skrzynski

# Child Cosmonaut

*Phillip Hatcher*


Child cosmonaut in steady incubation:
clad in turquoise jumper, a second skin,
hung and cradled by silver womb.
Not alone, just isolated
from all the other isolated.
This effort to rehabilitate the human race.
33 million compressions to restore humanity's heart.
Running from an attack of their own making.

The child's mind dances with sun-streaked rainy days
of their prior home, that pale blue dot.
They love the rain and are proud to become the rain.
A mineral bearing droplet of hope
to a green desert planet of nobody.
Minor understandings of falling with no pull nor gravity.
Just moving through time, utterly still.
Ghost echoes etch out the frame of a rose.
Bloomed white-static curves open for them.
Sprinkling bit of pollinated star seed.

A pulse of ions methodically projects

travel ever closer to voyage's goal.
An unknown environment besides
father's description: "hostile paradise."
Not fully conscious, they hear the engine.
Present and future rely on this device.
This ghost echo, the never beginning
and never ending heartbeat.
The heartbeat within.
The heartbeat of a species that
burned earth and bent light.
A heartbeat of arcane drums and screams.
A species that refuses to die in the dark.
Raging toward any way that will take them; or not.
Raging toward its own companion.
An entire entity of individuals, acting as one.
Something else that speaks in sounds and tongue.
Something that will record their existence.
That we were here, in this reality.
Only then will our flame finally fade.

# Metaphorical Door Slam

*Michele Steward*

I am so mad at everything sometimes,
"Why this? Why me? Why now?"
"What the hell did I do wrong?"
I'm considering all the meanings of "tanking"
And right now I'm taking a dive. The weight
Of one salty tear presses on my heart.

I hold my breath in fear. Who is that
Shouting like a maniac? Is that me shouting?
From a dark corner of my mind comes this RANT!
I am a scared, cowering pudding,
Hiding from my own indignation,
Gasping, barely remembering to breathe.

The clawing pain blossoms open,
Curiosity cures panic and I listen;
What am I so mad about?
I listen to the screaming child in me,
"I HATE this stupid world and the problems.
I have no control! No one asked me!"

"I don't want to play anymore! And
WHERE is a table for me to knock over?!"
I metaphorically slam the door.
Salt water leaks out of my face.
The weight of the tears burst.
Damned heart exploded.

I feel guilty about crying somehow,
Like I'm leaking poison or something.
Faced with that thought, it seems like a silly one.

I cry anyway and let go. The bottled fury stops yelling.
I can breathe again. Just breathe.

My salt water has not damaged the balance of the Earth.

# Background Radiation

*Tasha Jamison*


i told him that i'd spent the morning in a sensory deprivation tank
and he asked if i'd had an existential crisis

i wasn't sure what to say because it's not exactly
that i did or did not, it's just that, well,
"existential crisis" is the background radiation of my life

and i've spent my years learning the radioisotopes of anxiety,
the atomic weight of dread,
so that one day i can build my own thermal reactor
from the materials in my cabinets

last year the united nations convened a committee
gathering top researchers from nuclear agencies around the world
from hanford, chernobyl, goiânia, fukushima daiichi
they declared that there was no security threat to any of the world's
governments

but for safety's sake they built a containment unit for me
because lately every crisis nets a bigger reaction
so my angst generates heat

and the heat boils water
and the water turns to steam
and the steam is converted to electricity
and the electricity powers streetlights
and the streetlights…

i think i'm supposed to be content with this
i think i am not supposed to imagine revolution
i think i'm supposed to be satisfied that i am making lives better
i think i am not supposed to imagine the damage i leave behind

but i know that every day i burn brighter
and every day the hollows of my joints gain a little more space
and i know that there is safety for me in this water
but some days it's hard to breathe in the heat of my own body
when i know what happens downstream

# Insomniac

*Tanya Jarvik*

I used to date an insomniac. We never lived together, but we slept together often – or at any rate, I slept, and he occupied some nebulous, shifting state between restlessness and rest. I always fell asleep first, and usually woke after he did, although sometimes the alarm woke us both. This man claimed to sleep better with me than anyone else he'd ever been with, mostly because he never had to worry about his inevitable fidgeting disturbing me: I am a great sleeper.

Although we ended our three-year romantic relationship on relatively good terms, it's been almost two years since I saw him last. I rarely think of him, except to wonder why I don't miss him. But this morning, floating in the intensely salty water of a sensory deprivation chamber, zoning in and out of consciousness, I find myself remembering this former lover. I have my hands up near my head, my fingers tangled in my long hair, which feels like some kind of superfine seaweed, and I wonder what he would think of an experience like this: would he enjoy it, or would he find it intolerable? I imagine him, freed from the pull of gravity, buoyed up by salt water the same temperature as his skin, his ears submerged, his eyes open to the void....

My breathing changes. My heart rate speeds up. I'm

hyperventilating. I am actually panicking. Why? Because I do not want to feel things as I imagine him feeling them. I do not want to inhabit his reality. The uncomfortable, disconnected reality he escaped, when we were together, through me.

And now he's stuck without me.

Without me, he's stuck with a job he hates (but will never quit, even though he thinks about quitting every day). He's stuck with chronic fatigue. He's stuck with his endless search for the right diet – first, raw vegan; followed by macrobiotic; then paleo; followed by a whole month of nothing but liver, sweet potatoes, and fish oil. He's stuck with juice cleanses and colon therapy. Itchiness and irritation. A deviated septum. Too much phlegm. He's stuck with the bachelor pad he occupies, an aesthetic nightmare, with its concrete floor, painted cinderblock walls, and bad basement-window lighting. Clothes in piles on the floor of the closet. Wooden crates full of out-of-date self-help and woo-woo astrology books. An old boombox and a few forlorn cassette tapes. Dust bunnies. He's stuck with his superstitious regard for the I Ching. He's stuck with all the hours he wastes sitting in front of his computer searching for digital distraction, all that wretched, wretched porn. And without me, he's stuck with perpetual sexual frustration, porn notwithstanding, because his current life looks a lot like the life he led before he met me, and before he met me, he had spent almost his entire adult life alone, unless you count his engagement to a woman who refused to put out until they could sleep together, actually sleep, which was a joke, because she was also an insomniac: in seven years, they never once had full-on sex.

Holy mother of god, I think, how does he even *live?* (I hear his voice delivering that line, because it's clearly his exclamation, not mine: *Holy mother of god! He's still aliiiiive! It's a bloody miracle!*)

In the sensory deprivation tank, in a thought balloon that feels like it's actually taking up physical space somewhere just above my chest, a single word forms: GUILT. I don't see the letters; I sense them. And suddenly, I understand why it is that I hardly ever think about this man I once loved: because thinking about him makes me feel guilty. I feel guilty for leaving him. My life without him is far better than his life without me – or so I imagine; and that's the kicker, that's what really makes me feel awful: I've left him alone in the impoverished reality I've imagined for him, a reality I can't bear to experience, even in my imagination. Which means it isn't his reality, it's mine. I created it. And here, with nothing to distract me from this reality, I have no choice but to live it. I'm stuck feeling the way I imagine him feeling.

I'm stuck with him.

Ironically, as soon as I accept this, I begin to relax again. My breathing slows. My heart rate slows. When the music begins, letting me know my time in the tank is up, I feel refreshed, as though I've just woken from a deep and dreamless sleep.

# Light as a Feather

*Grace Totherow*

I have a stack of photos beside my bed. They're pictures of me throughout my life. Years ago I read a story about a woman who had such a stack of photos and would "work with them" each night before she went to sleep, sifting backwards through the years until she ended her session with an image of herself as an infant. Then she would go to sleep as the baby in the photo. That story tucked itself into the folds of my mind, and recently I decided to compile my own photos, one or two for each year of my life. Not knowing exactly what "work with them" means, I've decided to explore a bit. Starting with the most recent photo, I gaze for awhile at each one, allowing the essence of my memories to wash over me. As I track myself back through time, my belly tenses and releases in turn. I breathe and feel the stories flood my body and recede. . .flood and recede. I finally arrive at the photo where I am in my mother's arms at the hospital. She gazes with a content smile on her lips at my shock of black hair and dark eyes squinting under the lights. I turn the light off and roll onto my side, reach for my teddy bear and clutch her close, curling into myself. It must be twenty years now since I've slept with that bear.

Years ago I read a story about the initiation temples of ancient

Egypt. Before an initiate was allowed to pass on to certain levels of the path, their heart was laid on one side of a scale. A feather rested on the other. Only if those scales hung in balance could the initiate ascend to higher states of consciousness.

I have a friend who says she has a gift for seeing people's hearts. Images come to her of various materials that surround each heart. She may see a fortress of stone many feet thick, or a thin sheath of metal, or a series of walls made of wood. She told me she saw my heart bound with white cowhide. Soft and leathery, wrapped 'round and 'round, it created a tight bundle four feet wide.

I am unraveling this bundle. The ache in my heart for love, for home, is a familiar feeling. It floods my body and recedes. . .floods and recedes. In the silence and darkness of sleep, I sift through images. My heart floats on a sea of memories, longing to sink into peace.

# The World Behind Our Eyes

*Donovan James*

There is a world behind our eyes and there is a world of the senses. In our daily lives we seem to be lost in the former and fill the latter up with distractions – we are always doing something, but never appreciating what we're doing because we're lost in our thoughts. Existence seems to be too much of a burden for us, so we drink, we smoke, we check Twitter while watching Netflix – anything to relieve the responsibility of being a conscious human, even for only a couple minutes.

But what if we remove all sensory input and are left with only the world behind our eyes?

Our minds are free. Trains of thought speed along on different topics: dissecting our actions, our crude flirtations, our awkward comments (or hopefully, our charm, our kindness, our love). We can come to some level of understanding about these, about who we are, and plan to improve in the future.

But we can also take another step back and see the train for what it is: a series of thoughts that pop up in consciousness. We have some control over them, evidenced by how they're quieted and controlled after floating, meditation, yoga, and "good" psychedelic trips. But what becomes clear under these conditions is that thoughts are separate from consciousness (where consciousness is the totality of experience).

The physical effects of floating are unique. There's an infinite relaxation that absorbs you and becomes more than the sum of its components – how warm the water, how effervescent the pressure, how silent the world. When it's over, there's an odd sensation of returning to the body. In a vague sense, it's like getting back on a bike, except the bike is this ape avatar where you reside.

# Clovis (2016)

*Ken Pico*

Laces tied together
one loop, two, tenuously.
Feet compel me first to the window
where the edge of the world waits
over the balcony and beyond the horizon.

I draw the shutters to keep out the dark
yet am moved to venture into it anyway.
Feet compel me second to the door
and it click-locks on exit.
I find my way down
the weary, winding stairwell
a swift, urban gust kicking up for me.

After dusk,
the storefront windows seem lifeless:
cold mannequins and overdraft fees,
nail polish smeared on sterile tiles.
The leaves rustle so loudly at night
in the absence of the chattering
and it's got my attention.

In the warm glow
of lamp-lit concrete,
I see their reflections,
if only shadows, temporary,
in those stubborn mirrors
of shatterproof glass!
She is there among their figures,
plastic to flesh and vein shifting…
if only seemingly so.

A missed connection on a San Francisco bus
later becomes the crick-crick-crick
of a Ventures record perpetually ending,
driving at its leash stubbornly,
interrupted as lovers' songs continue to roll
across a naked twin mattress.

She is the closest I've ever seen of France
that glorious monument so skillfully etched,
the Seine still lapping
at the small of her back.

She was with me then,
two frantic teenagers,
all hands and skinny jeans,
knowing the train would soon
splinter the walls into rubble.
There was never a thought
it could be the last ticket home

before I was hauled back
into endless summer.

The memory transpires as hot steam,
covering closed car windows,
clouds that we created fervently
in rural parking lots
and drunken alleyway hideouts
until cop Maglites pierced
through the melting windows.
Then again in the back of movie theatres,
hushed for the sake of life or death.

She was all of them at once
yet none at all:
phantoms of a final Houdini act,
looping the prestige eternally...
her breath still raising hairs
at the nape of my neck!

Home again and curtains open.
I let nightfall linger for tea
as feet compel me to the window,
where the edge of the world waits
just over the edge of the balcony,
oozing over the banister to drip.
-Crick-crick-crick- goes the record
somewhere around a corner
where I still wait patiently
amidst this milky London fog.

# Embryonic Language

*Erick Mertz*

The sequence of things is where we go astray. Our routes back through toward the beginning start from the center summit. Downside of hill, one overlooking town from beneath a sandstone arch.

Our fingers have already traced the inscription identifying space.

Dusky light. The refugees of expectation. We breathed in stacks of sheet music, songs never once played and never heard. Like wind passing through tree branches overhanging the street corner where no one stands. There is a kitchen light on inside the house; there is a reading lamp. I can see the tilt of its shade.

The windows are closed. Those inside are confined.

One step forward. The air is light with passed-over song, caesura between tracks. These are the three seconds in which I can hear your footsteps, the rising wail of newness from down the hall.

I shift. The heart stop affirms something. Our union is a complicated assembly of these pauses, born in some other life. They are like a night thriving tendril, crawling forward blindly to the time when all those old mysteries had become replaced with those unread. Then the next song begins. I no longer hear you.

We have been reduced to commingling silences.

One step back from here. In a humid underground. Each song seamless with the one preceding. The one after elicits no pause in which to form an embryonic memory. You slide, slender shouldered, untouched through the mass. A figure of youth, born from the inescapable light.

When I say everything in the room became silent, I know this to be exaggeration. Silence consumed more than the room. Like a light reluctant vine, I retreated from the ceiling girders high above, training onto other neighboring branches, making my way toward.

I am reduced to the fate of knowing certainties.

Dusky light from here, back and forward. Wind passing through the branches where we fill in the corners. Cast shadow from the kitchen light. Do you see the reading lamp? The shade has tilted, better to read the words we've spilled across the page.

I throw open the window; although this move comes out of order, our mouths open willingly to consume the last moments of old confinement.

# Information Soup

*Michele Steward*

Simmer me eternally in Information Soup!
Nourishing, comforting the hankering
For curious wondering,
As I breathe in –
Information Soup.

Thickens with understanding,
Molecules, a tiny orbit of electrons,
Dancing with protons, neutrons,
Strong and weak forces...
Oh another helping!
Respire, inspire!
Lungs plucking oxygen,
Sending little care packets with my blood.
My beating heart, my bubbling soup rhythm!

Exhale, letting go,
I add my flavor to the brew.
As we all do.
These molecules intermingle with heroes
Through time. Einstein.

Mammals, dinosaurs, supernovae.
I let myself drink it all up.
We're all in the soup, brother.

And the moon is rich. The sun is rich,
That dense, layered, delicious mystery.
It's a savory reminder of our origins.

Over high heat, bring large pot to a
Big Bang.
When Space and Time separate, reduce heat to red hot.
Stir vigorously until clumps form and spread out.
Thin and cool this mixture until galaxies form on the edges.
Cover and reduce heat slowly,
Simmer until sentient beings just begin to form.

Watch the pot closely at this point.

Soup is now self-saucing.

Flavor to taste.

# Simultaneous:
# A Poem in Two Parts

*Tanya Jarvik*

I.
Stretched between sea and sky
swimming with stars and starfish, I
am simultaneous:
a photon spit from the sun
of a galaxy unnamed, unnumbered
and unknown to us
because it's just so far out there

there, there, there
and also not there

a million years awake
but fast asleep to time, so fast
traveling through constellations
indifferent to the stories we
still spin about them, dancing
around the puny fires of our cellphones

all the details of our dailyness

rimed over by inattention,
the way freezer-frost forms
on plastic ice cube trays,
or the way those neat white stripes
on a pair of red-and-white socks
begin to blush at the laundromat,
or the way one pearly curl of pasta
stuck to the bottom of a black pot
darkens and dulls, another question
picked off like a scab and thrown away.

## II.

Drifting in and out on the tide
of my own being, breathing out and in, I
am simultaneous:
wave and particle, sea and strand
universal and yet so unversed in the particulars
of other people's lives I might mistake
myself for one of them if I slide my hands
over the salt-slippery hills of my breasts
and feel them foreign,
mine and not mine

time and not-time
expanding and contracting
like this cage of ribs around my heart
and lungs, which I believe in, absolutely
though I've never seen them
or the oxygen they need, for that matter
tumbling around me every minute

while my thoughts, wrecked flotsam in my hair
soundlessly shush me

there, there, there
and also
not there.

# Time (2016)

*Ken Pico*


I shift listlessly,
weightless in darkness,
in a limbo
never explored.

My soul is a puddle
untethered, conceptual
silent vibrato
of a dissonant frequency.

Eager for expansion,
saliva is dripping from my jaws.
Yearning Nirvana wherever it reigns.

On an exhale and an embrace
I feel liberty in resistance,
feeling my sinews creak
joints releasing at ease,
an occasional twitch-kick,
pulsing relief through tired limbs.

I'm lingering carefully
on the meniscus between
fact and fiction,
between arbitrary definitions
depicting this experience.

Yet even here you linger,
somewhere nearby
in the shadows.
You won't let me leave!
My throat tightens,
sucking for air through parched pipes.
I want to cross over!
Give me the ethereal,
without your ceaseless ticking!
But you pin me,
like a faceless apparition
seductive and terrifying,
palms firm against my shoulders,
the face of a clock dangling,
only inches from my eyes.

Words of old advice
echo guidance
vague semantics of my curiosity
in this chamber of perpetuity.
"It takes time
to actually sound
like *yourself*."

Somewhere there
we're here together,
drawn outside the lines.
Fleeting vignettes,
canvasses crafted,
so deliberately carved
from the fingers of orchestra,
millennia,
crashing against its shores.

Eyelids blink?
But I can't draw
this blissful awe.
Rising on thirsty wings,
the only place I'm looking
is inward.

Illustraton by Levi Greenacres

# My Body is the Present, My Past is Underneath Me

*Jane Belinda*

I am floating
in a retrospective,
in a tank of my past.
It is saturated to the brim with salt.
I can see the pillars on the porch
of my childhood home,
the large oak tree in our backyard
that spiraled out from the overgrown grass,
the porch light swaying in
a breeze from days that have met it with more grace,
the popsicles sucked clean from the stick.
All of this is right in front of me
and all of this is made of salt
and all of this is dissolving away.

I am floating
the way stars float.
A pinprick in a dark blue sheet.
See how my light fingers out from my body
and grabs for more and more.

Like the night, I am calm.
This darkness does not scare me.
Light grows in every corner of my body.
In the pits of my elbows, in the corners of my eyes,
and in between my toes.
What is right in front of me is impossible to see
so I made myself into a beacon of light.
I am floating in the direction I was meant to go
to a place I cannot see yet.
I hope it is as nice as where I am now.

# What I Dreamed Of

*Aleks Stefanova*

I dream with my eyes open
I'm awake sometimes with them closed
Presence is found somewhere between what was and where I'd
like to go
There are stars blinking like curious eyelids within the ceiling
above me
Although night here, outside isn't even dark

I dream with my eyes open that someday, that soon
I'll build a world beyond magic
I tell myself daily "build it and they'll come"
Not sure yet who all I'd invite
All of you maybe, all of you here with me

I want kindness to guide us
I want peace to unite us
But somehow when there's no storm we all seem to get a bit bored
So look at that war that we construct
Look at our frail little bodies caught in the net of it all
Look at us bow to the fear of not having another day to love
someone

Look how it makes us all gravitate towards each other

I write love poems
I breathe in chaos, it burns like a salt gulp of ocean water
I exhale sorrow, there's not a soul that's not on fire out there
It makes me sick to know the cost of being loved
It makes me spit at the idea of unconditional

There's no cause without consequence
There's no reaction without the action portion
All there is, all there can be, is stillness
We live in a world that dances around itself, spins around an imaginary axis
Tell me you don't spin around from one harm to another
Tell me you don't wish to be held spellbound while you move restless like that
Tell me this
Why so restless? Why so afraid to be here under the microscope?
What do you gotta hide behind those pretty blue eyes?
Did you ever consider
This world was built by the fearless within you and me?

# Watching the Watchers

*Ben Ortlip*

I have the strangest sensation: of tall dark figures looming over me. Like a fish in a pond must feel looking out at a garden party. The figures aren't dark exactly, but of an otherworldly color I cannot distinguish from like shades; I can only see them as black on black. They look in on me, floating in my salty pond. They peer down at me as I peer up into their Vantablack assembly.

First, an exquisitely beautiful woman, the most human of the figures. Long flowing hair framing an unblemished face. Her skin so fair as to be reflective, the silvery haze of moonlight in her eyes.

Her features fade, smooth back into the velvet, and more faces appear, squirrely and squirming, peeking in and out over me. The movement frenzied, an amalgam of snouts and snarling lips: a soup-cauldron of the grotesque. The attitude here of inquisition, a malevolence held securely by a veil of indifference. The shapes care not for my life, my thoughts, my time. And yet, they watch me. They find an interest in me.

The swirling produces color – vivid scenes from my record of experience – and I flex my mental muscles, trying to steer the shapes in the darkness back into something I can understand. But this experience does not allow control. I release the mental tension holding me between these worlds and drift somehow backwards, deeper into my pond. Without eyes, I see the figures scatter and dash away, getting smaller as I fall.

The frame floods with movement, and I see the head of a giant-horned, scaled beast. It is looking at me, directly at me, and I feel that wave of curtained malevolence once more. A sense of "I am watching you" that is neither sinister nor comforting, but a cold truth to be accepted. Or denied and forsaken.

My body twitches and I wake up, feeling the passage of the hours, and the sudden movement in the stillness of the tank refreshes the sensation of temperature on my skin.

There is a different sense now. A sense of being here, now. Watching myself.

# Going In/The Water

*Andrew Nealon*

Hitchhiking...

Yeah I know. It's dangerous. But I think this is a dream so I'm just gonna go with it this time.

Walking on the side of desert highway can be a boring business...

This dream seems familiar. I think I'm trying to get up North, out of California. All the way up into the Oregon Mountains. So I'll take a ride from pretty much anyone as long as they are going that direction.

For long periods of time there is only moonlight. And stars. My phone died about an hour and a half ago. Six hours till sunrise. I think.

Nothing to do but wait for headlights... which pass about every hour. They leave me in darkness. At this time of night it's only getting darker and darker. And more silent as the space between the passing headlights gets longer. It's Summertime so I would imagine there would be a warm summer breeze, but there isn't.

It's getting weirder, I might be starting to hallucinate a bit... the desert is so different than the city. And time - the moments start to stretch out like... it seems like a single moment takes two beats... then three... and four like elastic...

I realize my breath is the only movement out here in all of this space. For miles and miles and miles and miles. I look around and see just these little lights out on the horizon, maybe a house or a city out there somewhere... but I don't know. It's kind of nice being out here alone.

There's time to just relax and think.

Dreaming starts so easily here. My mind wanders in this clear warm darkness. Ok so I know where I am now, I just passed a sign... and I'm registering it's about midnight. I know it's October 15th, my birthday, 2020.

Finally! I get picked up. Next thing I know I'm riding shotgun. The driver is quiet. So I just slip into a nice little nap, until the sun starts to rise and with the sun on my face I slowly start to wake, refreshed completely. Taking account of my surroundings I realize I'm in a SAAB. Possibly a SAAB from the 1990s. It's a convertible top, but the top and the windows are all closed up- the whole situation in the cabin of this car feels pretty air tight. I mean there is really some pressure in here, I can feel it in my face and neck and hands. Real quick I glance over before the driver realizes I'm awake, and I notice over the hand on the wheel- we are going well over 90 mph, explaining the air pressure - because when a SAAB gets going over 50 miles per hour it starts to tighten down on the suspension and everything else inside the vehicle with it, like a jet plane. We're going fast.

My second thought goes back to the dream I was just having: I was on a quiet beach in old Mexico. Listening to the singing bowls of Yogis. Then having dinner with my long passed grandmother, who we called Nana. We were at a formal black tie event that I promise you we only never actually attended, except of course, in my dreams, of wealth & expensive events.

I look over at the woman driving this vehicle at high speeds? She has some sort of magic quality, like a mermaid or a shaman...

The stereo speakers vibrate over the noise of the cars motor vibrations with something like psychedelic meditation music.

"Good morning" she says, moving one knee up and the other one down with the pedals. Clutch to the floor.

"Vrrrrmmm-Vrrrrrmm" she says to me out of a side smile...

Holy smokes. We were only in 4th gear? Right knee drops down again. Gently into 5th. Gas pedal back to the floor. 100 MPH plus now. Easily. The pressure in the cabin doubles.

"Open the door" she says, this time without moving a muscle or a bone in her face. It registers. She just spoke to me with her mind. Cool.

So I answer her, telepathically, of course, "Are you crazy? We're flying."

"Not the car door. Open the door of your mind, hitchhiker."

"Ok" I say, out loud.. with my mouth, it feels barbaric, but it's from the heart..

"Thanks" – mouth talking, and she side smiles again.

The windows start to "automatically" roll themselves down, literally, no one touched any buttons. The open windows let the superheated daytime desert wind into the cabin to blow our hair and our laughter around in every direction, for what seems like an eternity – and then some.

Hundreds of miles later, the SAAB still flying down the highway in the desert, and the sun is at high noon. It's hotter than ever so we stop at a motel to let the engine cool down, somehow. The motel is retro fitted, super tacky. An outdoor Hi-Fi that reminds me of the Flintstones is playing old time surf rock, mostly, and at least once some Moroccan jazz. The kidney bean shaped pool out front is the bluest, or, clearest water I've ever seen... The driver - I still don't know her name. But I loan her a t-shirt and shorts out of my bag so she can swim. After being in the water for some time, I finally telepathically ask:

"What's your name?"

"Holiday." She tells me with a timeless look.

Huh. I had a dog named Holiday, just a few years ago.

"Are you ready to go in the water?" She asks.

I think to myself, "Yes!"

But, honestly, I realize I'm dreaming and I've been in the water for over an hour...

And suddenly it's night time again, pitch black, and I'm waiting for headlights, and everything is as it should be.

Illustraton by Levi Greenacres

# Wake Engine V.3 Customer Review

*Greg Elderidge*

In the enveloping evening peace that the Wake Engine brought me, I saw who I was for the first time. As if millions of faeries were floating 'round in the room of my consciousness, I saw with my spirit – in other words, was – the several excitations of a field blazing: burning light. It was my fourth time being in the third and newest version of the Wake Engine; they've buried all evidence of the technology which makes the machine work. In other words, they've found a way to forgo the plastic, the wires, even the outer shell of the pod itself, and now you enter but a room as any room, and it's as if for a moment nothing has changed.

And nothing has changed except who you know yourself to be, and that, of course, changes everything. It turns you from a clown who takes it seriously when someone honks its red nose into a clown who's in the know and laughs. Since the invention of the Wake Engine, the world has been but a mad rush of clown energy, ravenous to learn how to laugh at the joke of it all, and this new machine has you hysterical in less than an hour.

They say – and I now know it to be true – that the more one goes into the Wake Engine the more one gets out of the Wake

Engine, exponentially, and that with this new third model, the change comes much quicker than with the previous ones. As one got more accustomed to the earlier models' claustrophobic case, dim techno-lighting, and inexplicable multifaceted tubing structures draping from above the ceiling to below the floor, it became easier to relax and let go, to succumb to the muscle of the machine into which one walked, to trust the professional whose hands one was in – all vital for a successful Know. With these features gone, the machine exposes no semblance of its engine, of whatever makes a Know work, the natural effect of which is that one is less conscious of where one is and what one is doing and so erects fewer walls between the mind and the technology, between one's normally perceived false self and one's true self, or that of which one goes to the machine to become aware. Obscuring the mechanization was the cleverest advance in technology since the invention of the Wake Engine itself, twenty years this Sunday's prior.

And now! (And I say now though it happened last night, as last night I experienced for the first time a different kind of "now," which I am certain is connected with this one.) Now I have no justification for a penny of incredulity regarding the 3's illustrious new slogan: "We'll show you God or your money back!" With this new model speeding up the initial ego-death part of the experience, most people won't have any reservations about finding themselves exposed, and God, Inc. can make such a claim. The great irony is that everyone made a mockery of God, Inc.'s name and claim until the company started showing people who they really were. "The customer is never right," it's rumored the employees were trained. "If the customer complains, then the machine didn't work for him or her, but that, to put it subtly, is not the fault of our machines." And now with this third model, everyone has the opportunity to understand what this means, and employees don't need to be trained anymore. People no longer need any spiritual guidance, any faith, reasoning, discipline, obedience, piety, or even belief. Laugh as you will, but anyone can find God with the right amount of money.

Everyone enters the Wake Engine expecting to learn something, to find something out. The only thing one discovers, however, is that one did not go in to learn, but rather to unlearn. And unlearn is what the machine will make one do – all the way until one perceives as a baby again. With such a fresh and strong memory of the perspective of a newborn baby, which cannot be achieved though anything other than the Wake Engine (and some people say years of deep meditation, but I suggest forgoing the difficulty and spending the cash on a Know), the mind adopts that perspective for the rest of its life, allowing the crisp awareness of the universe perceiving itself through the mind instead of the usual perspective of the mind perceiving the universe through itself.

This illumination cannot be shaken off. It is not some transient effect. Not everyone commits to entering the machine, out of a fear of the outstanding change that results. But I admit now for the first time: I had my own fears of what might happen when the day comes when there isn't a soul that isn't conscious of the universe being self-conscious, or what God, Inc. calls, and some ancient mystics called, the embodiment of pure awareness. If everyone in the world is aware he's nothing but the court jester, what becomes of the court?

Now, after last night, it is clear to me: The court too is a game, and if we're all laughing jesters and the court turns into a circus, then we've entered a new age in the history of human civilization, and we were heading there all along. The biological evolution of human life, the inception of agriculture, and the resulting mighty thrust of technology, science, and slow forging of capitalism and globalization were all in the original plan – all leading to God, Inc. and finally the invention of this third version of the Wake Engine, which will soon bring about world peace and a time in which the clown paint is visible beneath all of our skins. In this way consciousness is evolving to become aware of its self-awareness in order to save itself though its own kind of natural selection. If the clowns take their nose-honking too seriously, after all, then the honks are heard as grave alarms instead of the silly sounds they are and the universe loses its self-awareness. Only through experiencing the dualistic perversion of thought as nothing more than a social institution could the humans and other clever jokers of the universe laugh enough to avoid self-destruction.

5 stars out of 5 for the Wake Engine V. 3.

# Huixtocihuatl: Salt Water Goddess of the Aztecs

*Michele Steward*

She must cry an ocean.
Mighty tidal emotions of global importance,
A crushing tsunami throwing boats onto once-dry land
And ripping up trees and houses from their seemingly strong roots.

A force to be reckoned with, she will wreck you.
A saltwater embrace swallowing all.
Yet she is a goddess of fertility.
Dragging, raking, washing the land
Her embrace means life.

Who would drown the goddess?
She gives her salty blessings unending.
Celebrate, dance, and make a sacrifice in her honor.
A tribute of salt,
And the heart of a woman.

# Initiation

*Grace Totherow*

Morning meditation. This is a simulation. I remind myself again. A simulation. A holographic illusion, pixilated impressions, fractals cracking moment by moment. Subatomic particles in my mind-body react to and impact, in rapid succession, these flickering shadows on the temple walls.

Just watch. I remind myself again. Be still. Breathe. Observe. Waves of heat pour over me. I sweat. My left knee aches like a knife's been shoved into my ankle. Be still. It will change. It always does.

I'm not sure how long I've been here. Maybe a week, maybe a few hundred years. In these temples, one can't really tell. Time is eclipsed within the images that spit across the temple wall screen displaying every fear I can possibly dream. My mind shrieks, whimpers, growls, wails, keens in endless cycles of raging triumph and defeat.

Afternoon initiation. First time I tried this one I failed, but I didn't die.

A group of us stands in a circle around a hole in the stone floor, full of water, not quite a square yard wide. One at a time, we enter this hole of water and swim downward. We've been training for this. Weeks, months, years of meditation and teachings.

My turn. One breath. Having tried and failed once, I know how to navigate the early stages. Full awareness every moment. Enter the water with caution. Pay attention. There it is, the first one, a few feet down. A granite slab. Hard and shallow enough to crack my skull wide open if I dive in too fast. I duck around it, swim deeper. Here's the second one. Swim around it, go deeper. Must be at least twenty feet down now. The tunnel opens to an underwater chamber. I look up and see a wide circle of light far above. There they are. Crocodiles. I don't panic like I did before. And I learned last time that if I swim pass the crocs to the light and climb out of the water, I will fail again.

There is another way out. One breath. I'm scared. Fear in my belly, in my heart. My lungs ache like ancient grief. I turn my eyes away from the light above and focus deeper into the darkness. I swim down. My hand touches stone. The bottom? Yes? Yes! I swim forward, fingertips clawing stone. Pitch black. I'm blind. Go by feel. I can't breathe. Stay aware. I'm going to die. Be here.

Suddenly the floor drops away and my hands reach and grasp only water. Go deeper. Pay attention. I'm scared. I'm dying. There's no way out. Go deeper. Again my hands find stone and I pull myself forward. Careful. Stone wall. Channel moves up. Utter darkness. Careful. Stay aware. Is this the way? Swim upward. Pitch dark. Granite slab. Recognize the patterns. I've seen this before. Upward. Another slab. Upward. Patch of light above. My lungs burn, ready to explode. I ignite a fuse of pure will within to catapult my body through the last few feet of water. My head breaks the surface and I gasp, open-mouthed, groan in my first breath. With shaking arms, I pull myself out, lay on the stone slabs and sob. My body heaves and trembles. My tears mix with the Nile's waters, trickling in rivulets on the temple floor.

Evening meditation. Moments of grace like this do come. I bathe in their ease and relief, feel my body composed of stars, clustering in constellations of organ, muscle, and bone. Light washes over me, steeps in every cell. Seven seals spin with precision. Music of spheres resounds within my temple. Songs of the cosmos roll in waves from root to crown. Harmonics, resonance, hues of gold, silver, pink, stream along the energy lines, lighting up my heart with joy and peace.

Tonight I sleep deeply and dream.

Tomorrow we will begin again.

Illustration by Mike Skrzynski

# The Water Witch

*C. Starling*

The pool at the bottom of the cave was quiet and still.

Nothing grew down here. There was no kelp to snare her ankles, or crabs to scuttle beneath her and stir the mucky sand. There was only her, and the water, and the salt, and the darkness.

She stretched out her fingers and took a deep breath. Far above her, water dripped and bats roosted. She'd seen them on her way down. But from here, she couldn't hear them. She couldn't even see the rocks that jutted out above the pool, forming a half-ceiling.

The water had started out cold but had quickly warmed from her skin, and after half an hour, she'd slithered out of her heavy clothing. The salt clung to her, crusting on her belly where it rose above the surface, spidering up the underside of her jaw. She breathed in again, smelling the faint brine scent. She'd always thought of herself as a child of the ocean, but now she knew it went deeper than that.

This darkness nestled in her breast like it belonged there. Like she belonged here.

Outside the cave, a storm raged. She'd taken shelter high above a day ago. But the sun had set and risen again still masked by howling clouds, and she'd been unable to look out towards her home across the cove, savaged by the winds. She'd retreated inside, leaving her boat tethered close by, and she'd climbed down, trying to block out the sounds. She'd found the pool by chance, and she'd been floating now for hours.

Slowly, her thoughts had expanded past the rock around her.

She felt the churning of the ocean the same as she felt the rhythm of her pulse. She focused on that thought, and felt them come closer and closer together, matching one another. She heard the roar of the storm like she heard her breath leaving her nostrils, and slowly she damped the fury down to match the quiet whisper of air. And she knew, somehow, that the ocean had listened.

The storm was over.

Still, she floated on. Soon, she'd climb out of the water and go back to her boat, she'd go find the wreckage and help rebuild, but for now, the pool was all she needed. She was safe, wrapped up in the blanket of black. Here, her thoughts could dance in a way they never could in her small fishing village. Here, her thoughts could reach the stars and bring down pockets of light to spiral behind her closed eyes. The sounds of her body grew into music, ghostly music that she couldn't hear, but could feel.

The darkness simplified everything. She was a child again, her thoughts exploring off to the right of her, then above her. She tracked them idly, smiled as she followed the sensation of peace they left in her wake. Even when she thought of her dirty, tiny home, even when she thought of the uncertainty of her future, even when she touched on the parts of her life that should have been nothing but raw nerves, she was insulated from it. She could see it, hold it, let it go again.

She'd never felt so in control, or so safe. She'd never felt as a part of herself, or floating so far above.

If the sea called to her again like this, she'd answer.

No – that wasn't it. The sea was always calling.

When she needed this again, she'd return. She'd make the difficult journey that she'd made only as an accident the day before, cut off from home by the growing swells. She'd learn the path. And she'd stretch out across the blackness, breathe in, and expand outwards. The salt would crust her nails and give her power, and she'd be as she now knew she'd always been – powerful, safe, and joyful.

It was all there; she only had to listen to the darkness.

# The Woman is an Ocean

*Michele Steward*

Falling backwards, tip my head,
Weird, but it felt good instead.
I'm a little teapot, pour me out!
Open my head, release all doubt.

Let it go, wiggle it free!
Eyes are open, nothing to see.
Eye the prize inside instead,
Living, waking, dreaming, dead.

This little vessel is "me" for a while,
I weave the threads, I cut this style.
From basic fiber fabrics grow.
Who sees threads when costumes show?

Best for someone to mind the seams,
Mend them into tattered dreams.
Densely woven cloths for sails,
And fine, raw silks for virginal veils.

Don't lose the thread! A fishing net,

I've got a catch! Full, salty, and wet.
Mind the tension! Mind the knots,
Best repair those on the spot.

Ride, ride: life, winds, and tide.
Be a consummate lover to life's blushing bride!

# A Galaxy Dreams of Being Human, A Tree Dreams of the Stars

*Jane Belinda*

I am not one for looking up at the sky
trying to find something that can't be found on earth.
There are already aliens living behind my eyes.
There are already black holes in my wrists.
Planets rest in the temples of my skull.
This body is the smallest galaxy.
I am always searching for something
that will glue this planet to me more,
to be grounded like roots.
I find myself unmovable
like a tree grown in a planter box
a perfect square of laced-together pulp.

But I wish I was a dreamer
or a star gazer.
I wish I could untangle myself from myself
be a person, not a galaxy, or knotted-up roots.
I could float away in imagined spaceships

to places where I weigh nothing,
to places where nothing is weighing me down.
Everyone is looking for reasons to float away
to unhinge themselves from reality,
to become the star that is farthest away
from where we are standing.
Reality exists in the moments
we are not even thinking about it,
when we are simply floating in it all.
If only we could get this weight off our backs.
If only we could all be dreamers.

# The Rude Awakening of Bernie Cheeseman

*Greg Elderidge*

The awareness of Bernie Cheeseman lay in Bernie's bed, split between the light that broke in the new day through his window – with what early morning might could be mustered – and his pondering of the best way to wake himself up enough to get out of bed. Soft German vibrato eased in from his smart alarm clock, breathing familiar consciousness now into his routine dread of the morning battle of transitioning into the waking day. Bernie's awareness (which, for sake of brevity, will henceforth just be called Bern, while his ego we'll name Dutin, and his body Chuch) of the Bavarian tremolo infuriated Dutin, who tried in vain to kick the insulting sound waves back out of the eardrum.

"You go away," Dutin yelled. "Chuch isn't ready to hear that – he's still tired, can't you see?"

Bern heard Dutin's cry and then felt Chuch's tired arm reach blindly toward the Deutsch lungs and squelch them breathless with a press of the snooze button. Ten-minute suicides Monday through Friday – three of them each good morning.

Homicide too, thought Dutin. Morning fatigue turns the countertenor into a Nazi; we'll have two more battles before I silence the kraut.

Bern shifted to Dutin's desire to shield the encroaching morning light from Chuch, lest it keep them all awake and render the 'spuicide' naught but a failed attempt. Chuch turned over, burying his eyes in the blackness of the pillow.

Nothing more shameful, Dutin thought, escaping the indignity with a swift drift back to sleep.

Here Bern ceased to exist for a divine ten minutes, and Dutin and Chuch followed suit. There was nothing, not even darkness or the perception thereof, and all parts of Bernie Cheeseman's perceived existence – inner and outer – simply weren't.

"Du, feines Täubchen, nur herein!"

Bern was always the first of the three to awaken, but Dutin was always the first of the three to react. Like most days, Dutin turned the libretto into dread and, soon after, into an internal growl of expletives and obscenities. This in turn convinced Chuch, who wanted nothing other than to silence a distraught Dutin, to use what was seemingly all of his energy to throw his arm down, again, somewhere around the alarm clock. Dutin prayed the arm would carry out the homicide in one smooth, instant kill. But instead the hand fumbled, naked in the darkness around the desk, receiving no aid from Chuch's bolted eyelids.

"O, welch Marter! Welche Pein!"

The floundering hand frustrated Dutin enough to convince Chuch to expose his eyes to the breaching dawn. Chuch was farther to the wrong side of the bed than thought and lamented his need to roll over to reach the blessed doze switch. The pupils of Chuch's bare eyeballs tapered at first communion with the daybreak light, rendering Bernie's shift back into slumber problematic. With another snooze came a new silence, within which Dutin could savor every moment, and though Chuch drifted to sleep, Bern became ever more alert. Now Bern felt for the first time a strange, new perception: Chuch was numb in the command of sleep, but Dutin continued on in the waking day, unswayed by Chuch's inertia. Bern, aware now of a sleeping body and a stirring ego, knew for the first time a floating consciousness somehow separate from the body.

"Verloren ist dein Leben!"

But stubborn Chuch would not awake.

Dutin knew, now, that it was time for Bernie to wake up once and for all and get out of bed. Bernie needs to get dressed! Dutin thought. Bernie needs to wake up and brush his teeth! Put on the coffee! Go to work! Bernie can't be late again, Dutin thought. Bernie will be fired. But now the German breath wailed on and he could do nothing to stir Chuch from his limpness! Was this death – a paralyzed Chuch and a tortured Dutin caught in a rancorous round? Consciousness lived on detached? A rude hell!

Contrariwise, without ability to respond to his body, to any sensations, impressions, or feelings, at last maybe the mind would learn to find peace. Yes, his body would be gone, and the Nazi snuffed out along with it. Death does not move me; only my mother will mourn for me. She will die of grief most certainly.

Der Tod macht mich nicht beben,

Nur meine Mutter dauert mich.

Sie stirbt vor Gram ganz sicherlich.

Bernie Cheeseman woke up. He turned off the alarm, brushed his teeth, and put on his suit.

As he poured his coffee, he wondered who Bernie Cheeseman was.

# Floating Around And Round

*Andrew Nealon*

I heard the ancients say...
Welcome back into this darkness.
It's connected in here.
There is depth in here.
In this place is deep space, the womb, gravity, the ocean–
All of the most powerful elements... exist in nature, in depth, and
often in total darkness...

In here they are all connected to You.
And your internal stillness... and your naturally occurring rhythms.

So  –  In here...just–
Stop. And...
Breathe. And…
And experience this connection–

(Do yourself all the favors, and Re-read that)

Breathe…
Breathe…
Breathe...

Imagine your body is the ocean.

And just like that...

You are.

You are absolutely everything ocean now;

Swelling, as you inhale, you are the tide pulling back it's force.

Exhaling, you are the crashing waves, crushing rocks into sand.

Floating, filled with your dreams, you are the infinite schools of fish, in an infinite depth.


Now, further you go – out into the Cosmos, just to see what you can see...

Imagine you are the moon.

And just like that...

You are.

You are floating around the earth, seeing everything;

Inhaling you are rising, waking up the owls for work.

Exhaling you are all the sleeping people dreaming;

Master of the world's imagination,

Floating around and round,

Your have nocturnal vision.


Now imagine you are the Earth...

You ARE that pretty little blue dot, floating, in the darkness;

...Floating, get it?!


A planet floats in space, just like a baby floating in the womb.

From macro to micro, infinitely connected.

So now imagine You are You – but before being born;

Just a floating micro-organism – with no concept of self;

From the very first cellular vibration you felt,
Before all the newness even started,
Before the Sun light changing on our faces triggered deep emotional
reactions,
When we were more like a sea anemone – than a human being;
Just a simple organism floating in a pool of water,
Serving the ecosystem, part of the world on the most basic level.
And that was you –
Then & Now.

Wake up.
Turn on the lights.
Was it all just a dream?
Do you remember, maybe... a single moment?
The one that will last forever in your memory box?

Well... Maybe remember this,

You are always floating –
Just like you always have been,
And always will be...

So, Breathe

# Me, Leaving a Message on the Float Tank's Voicemail, A Love Triangle: Part I

*Nikki Burian*

Hey, it's me. Leave a message. *beep*

Hi. I just wanted to let you know, the past few Monday afternoon dates we've been having…well…they've changed my perspective on things, really.

I like you.

I like the weightlessness I feel when I'm with you. I don't know how to explain it. You make things better. You make me want to be better.

I know last time we hung out, I told you about Anxiety, how we've been dating for quite a few years now.

I think she knows I've been seeing you.

Maybe she'll be okay with this, as long as I come home to her.

I have always gone back to my Anxiety.

I have always built a life within her; she's always there when I have nothing left.

It's just easy, y'know? It's easy to remain when staying is all you've ever known. Does it make sense not to leave something terrible because you can't remember anything else? I don't know…now I'm just talking to myself.

But then I met you and it's as if…as if Anxiety never knew my name.

I want you to know that I'm thinking of leaving her.

I might need help…I'm not sure. I just…I know how I am when I'm with you. I know how I am when I'm with her.

The three of us cannot love this way for much longer.

I need you. I can't wait to see you again.

Call me when you can.

# My Anxiety, Leaving a Message on the Float Tank's Voicemail: A Love Triangle, Pt. II

*Nikki Burian*

Hey, it's me. Leave a message. *beep*

I had a feeling this would happen.

I think I knew it, actually.

I make my living as a gut feeling, y'know, I am so used to being the person who makes the right decisions to keep Nikki prepared and safe.

We've done this for years…she'll get overwhelmed and I take over, shut her down, get her to stop everything she's doing so she can focus on me. I've had a good life. This is how it should be.

Then you come along, and she starts to fight back.

At first I thought this could work, y'know, she always comes back… but I haven't seen her in weeks now.

I don't understand. You and I are the same.

We both deprive her of her senses and yet YOU'RE the one she keeps drifting back to. How do you do that?

How do you give her a reason to be better by taking everything away from her? How do you soothe? How do you provide?

This isn't fair.

If she goes, if she really leaves me, I won't be there to make her second-guess her decisions. She will be forced to have the courage to stand up for herself and create her own happiness.

I can't let that happen.

I have been taught to uproot and uproar. If you take her from me, I will be nothing – maybe we can work something out.

Call me.

# Dear Body

*Rooze Garcia*

Dear Body,

I know I said this would be the year that I made you a priority, that I focused on health and drank more water and walked more miles. I told you that once I had health insurance (woo-hoo, Obamacare!) I'd start getting things taken care of. And I've been true to my promises. Mostly. (The water thing really is harder than it sounds; I mean, at 43 years old, you would think I would already know how to drink enough water every day.) I wish you would have trusted me and not gone into full-blown meltdown just to make sure you became the priority. Although, after decades of crumbling resolutions, I sort of understand your skepticism.

But here's the thing. I can't take much more of this pain. A month without NSAIDS and it feels like there's a metal rod in my left hip and a crew of tiny jackhammers chipping away at my lower back. This would be easier to deal with if I knew it was going to get better. I need for you to chill out more often than just when I'm in the float tank or listening to binaural beats. Please?

They – the doctors, the specialists, the folks online in various support groups – say that there's no cure for this new diagnosis. I can hope for remissions. I can enjoy moments of being able to move and stretch and not cry. They promise me that will be true.

At some point. For some unknown duration. I guess we both need to learn trust, you and I.

There was a time once that we swam in the warm waters of the Gulf of Mexico, then floated under the bright Floridian sun, supported by the salinity of the ocean. We were one then; you and I would stretch our arms, and thought and body moved as one. Fluid motions, no resistance, no grit. That's how we grew up, remember? And the long bike rides, the way these legs would propel us into freedom and safety, away from the craziness of our house.

Remember how we'd dance in dark clubs, loud music thumping through us, pumping our motions? We'd get as close to the speakers as we could to feel the sound waves pulsing against our heart. Exhausted, we'd sleep a hard-earned sleep and wake up with the kind of satisfied soreness that brought smiles rather than frustration. Those were the years. I didn't think we were leaving them behind. Like in a warm tub slowly cooling, suddenly I find myself surprised to be shivering.

Don't think I've forgotten how you were there when my mind wasn't; how you kept on getting us through each day while I struggled to find a way through the cracks and back into sanity. I think of that often these days, how odd it is for my mind and spirit to be stronger than you. Maybe together we can all pull through this? It isn't bliss I need, just more moments of peace than of pain.

If I keep telling you how magical you are, will you ever again believe me?


Yours,


Me.

# The Consequences of Floating

*Sione Aeschliman*

## 1

The first little while is always about coming back into my body.
Becoming un-numb.

Breath and heartbeat. Water lapping against skin. The muffled roar
of the inside of my head.

Eventually my consciousness expands beyond close boundaries to
include the rumble of a truck passing on the street, a fellow floater
bumping in their tank.

Then the un-work begins. Time passes, barely acknowledged.

When I step out, my body fits me better. Or perhaps I fit better in
my body.

Taut skin and soothed muscles, with as much coordination as a
new colt.

Pleasantly fuzzed without the hangover headache, my mind is a
lazily churning eddy in a clear, warm stream.

## 2

After several risings and sinkings of consciousness, abrupt awareness
that my knees and shoulders are still bound up. Do they ever fully
relax?

Now I catch myself tensing my left knee when it has nothing to
do. While I'm driving. Or sitting in bed. Lounging with friends on
a bar-side patio.

And all day my shoulders knit themselves into knots, frozen in a half-shrug. It takes conscious effort to reseat them, and when I check back half an hour later, they've migrated back upwards again.

## 3

Let go.

It's the first thing I center on when I'm in the tank, and my new mantra outside it.

I breathe it into my muscles.

Whisper it silently when I'm afraid someone will feel angry or think less of me if I tell them my truth.

Or when I feel the internal fires of jealousy, anger, shame. Instead of trying to bind, dismiss, or bury what disturbs me, I want to let go of the barriers separating me from my experience, me from myself. I want to let it come. I want to remember to forget to put up the walls.

## 4

I am a tightly clenched fist. So tightly clenched and for so long, it's painful to open. Not a release, a prying apart. Rusted metal squealing.

I want this, and yet I am terrified. If I let go, what will keep me from flying apart? My atoms, forgetting their purpose, will rush out with eager curiosity to explore the corners of the universe.

If I let go, I cease to be what I am.

## 5

I imagine curling my body to the side and, without any conscious effort on my part, my body curls to the side. Movement as easy as thought. The water slides deliciously, tantalizingly over my skin. A unique sensation, a slither-caress. Enchanted, I imagine curling to the other side, and again my body glides. I play for a while, encouraging the sensation, reveling in the ease of movement without conscious effort.

6

When all the emotions pile on top of me and I can't breathe
or I'm lying in bed, my body rigid with worries
I imagine I'm in a float tank.
Immediate, the sense of relief.
An external space internalized,
I carry with me a source of calm.


7

Lying in the warm dark, merged with water, I imagine leather-and-
metal braces covering my body. I've worn them since childhood – I
made them myself – thinking they'd keep me safe and stable. Instead
they limit my movement and chafe me raw.
One by one I unbuckle them and let them float away.
Unbound.
And it occurs to me that now I am Unbounded too. Without
boundaries. Limitless.
I do not know what the consequences will be; I recognize only the
possibility of becoming.

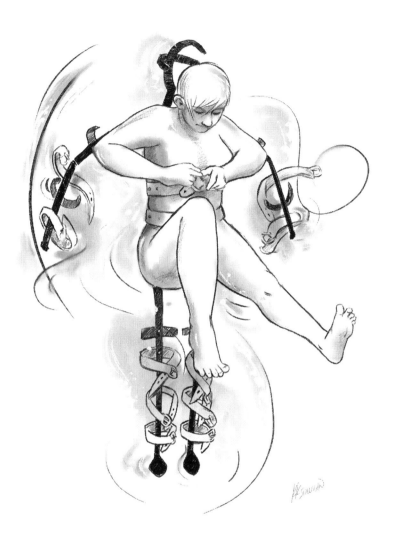

Illustration by Kathryn Sullivan

# When Seen from These Angles

*K.C. Swain*

I became something else. With this final float I decided to focus on a single thought and think my way into it. I knew there would be an infinite number of thoughts racing around my consciousness, but I wanted to see what happened when I focused my energy towards a single idea or form.

Once I settled in and let the gravity go, I realized my upper body was where the work needed to be done. Maybe it wasn't so much about the thoughts, but more about what I could do with my physical form once I separated my waking and physical selves. The whole process felt like the top dropping down on an old Cadillac. Slowly but surely I started to dissolve physically. The flashes of light began, and my being started to barrel down a dark familiar tunnel.

Traveling through my body to combat the pain and stress, I saw it. It was like watching The Magic School Bus, when Ms. Frizzle and the kids go inside the human body to explore germs. They fly in through a cut on Ralphie's leg. I did a version of this. I instead snuck in through my mind, through the electrons, protons, and neutrons at the speed of light. So fast I forgot where I was.

I saw the tissues of my body and the electricity. At first it seemed like I was sliding down a giant fleshy tunnel so fast I couldn't make out the actual images. It was lightspeed in the Star Wars universe but a lot darker, as though someone had forgotten to turn the Millennium Falcon's headlights on. I traveled toward a bright light in the distance. It led me to the pain and stress in the deep stretches of my neck and shoulders. I have always wanted to take a peek inside the hurt parts. If I can see the problem instead of just feel it, maybe I can fix it. I saw myself pushing ligaments back into their alignments and pinching a trigger point in my fascia tissue until it released.

I became the physical therapist to my dreams and lived experiences. Able to pull the problem from one angle and then work the tissues like a savage in another. I was seeing myself inside out. I focused all my energy on becoming in tune with the problem areas, literally taking on their form so I could release them and soothe them. I thought my way into my muscles and the physical stress connected to mental stress.

I became hyperaware of the interconnectedness of the body and its trigger points. It made sense because I could see these processes happening while also feeling them. The float helped kick-start the process of healing and helped me realize I'm the energy that can ultimately maintain itself.

I was seeing in 4-D. I could see the physical stress as wounds, and see the how wounds appear in my mind's eye. The actual manifestation of stress: talking to my Dad about my long-lost sister, and studying for this damn Language Arts content test so I can be a teacher were the knots in my back. From one angle I saw these images as they are in waking life, but then from another angle I now saw them as balled-up tissues and misfiring electrodes. The wires were mixed up, and from a different angle I saw how to unwind them and let them flow again.

It was a collection of all my stress, physical pains, and lessons learned.

I floated to the left and saw the stress from sitting at my computer typing a research paper, creating lesson plans, and sitting for hours reading article after article. It was strange to see stress in 4-D, it seemed less of a burden and easy to fight. Easy to let go like a balloon.

This feeling of releasing and doing the dirty work only built over the duration of the session. Each moment building on the last until the lights slowly came on and the music vibrations tickled me awake.

Illustration by Liliya Drubetskaya

# Doors in the Sky

*Carly Jean*

Invited to experience a salt water float last-minute, my answer is an easy yes. I have journeyed deep inside during Inipi a handful of times, and those ceremonies pushed me a long way out of comfort before retrieving me. I needed them, as I need this. I feel more curious than fearful about sensory deprivation.

Naked and rinsed, I close the tank door behind me and slosh into the dimly lit pool. Crouching down and immersing myself slowly in the water, I recline and dip my head back, feeling the water take hold of my hair and reverberate it in small waves. As soon as I'm settled in the pool, weightlessness reaches my consciousness and I feel relief. Air bubbles pop noisily out of my ears and warm, salty water backfills the canals. I reach over and turn the dim lights out, easing myself into darkness. I try a couple of positions with my arms floating at my sides, then overhead. Soon I am mostly comfortable and remind my stubborn neck to relax more, tipping my head back enough to immerse most of my face, the waterline encircling me and exposing just my nose and mouth to the humid air.

The next thing I notice is the sound of breathing. Along with my thudding heartbeat, it is quite loud now, and I think about how babies might hear their mothers' hearts and lungs just like this in utero. My thoughts skip around erratically like lightning bolts, and soon my mind tires of its own compulsivity. After a while, raw emotions float up. Anxiety blights the mental and emotional landscape inside. Work stress intrudes unpleasantly, and so does the ensuing ego struggle of *am I good enough, are all the problems my fault, will things ever get better, did I do everything wrong? Am I all wrong?* Eventually my preoccupations fall away and I realize with a great deal of relief that I am a solid state under all the agitation. Something about the supportive water and the rhythm of my heartbeat cuts through the choppy waves above to reveal that none of that nonsense is real, and I am whole and healthy down here. I begin to lose a sense of time, and the blackness inside and outside of me merge into an expansive peace. It is time to journey now.

I open my mind's eye, and see a late-winter garden with nothing growing in it. *Is this my garden?* – Yes – I hear. I approach a raised bed and plunge my hands into the soil. *Can I grow something here?* – Yes, but you must clear the soil first – . So I rummage around in the black earth for a while. Wet with heavy soil, my hands collide with hard things and I start to pull them out of the bed and set them down on the ground. They are bones. Skulls, arm bones, leg bones, bony hands and feet. Dismembered beings that beg to be re-membered. I dig until there's nothing left, and collect the sad bones in my arms. I set them down on a potting bench and begin to dust off the soil, revealing the clean white surfaces beneath. I tell them I'm sorry they have all come apart, and start to cry. I weep because I don't know how to put them back together. I weep because chaos reigns even in the blackness. My tears wash them clean and they begin to self-organize, to reassemble, to re-member. I stand back as they become partial-bodies, half-bodies, then eventually, there are several whole bodies there. The skeletons blink and fade and then become people dressed in clothes, wearing glasses, walking around together slowly. I realize they are my ancestors, my kin. We have waited a long time to be reunited. I am filled with grief and know that I must speak to each of them, must face them all. One by one, they approach me and look into my face with love. They whisper messages lighter and softer than summer wind, and in soothing tones advise me they have brought me gifts to remember them by, as I must let each one go to the great beyond forever. They need me to liberate them.

My maternal grandfather gives me a pocket watch. Maternal grandmother, a spatula. Paternal grandfather, a pocket knife and a hatchet; paternal grandmother, a shell or whalebone hair comb. My older brother gives me a harmonica and my little sister gives me a colorful lollipop. With each approach, I memorize their faces with my curious hands, then hug them tightly as one by one they whisper – goodbye – . Each ancestor wanders over a grassy hill to a door in the sky. They open their doors, enter the light, and then close the sky behind them. I cry hard and the rush of pressure into my ears and sinuses is very loud. So are my sobs, which echo in the float chamber and threaten to shake me out of my reverie. I sink back into the scene and realize it is, at last, time to face my parents and let them go, but my psyche resists. *Next time, maybe, I can face them.* – No, it is time, and you can do it – . So I wait, and they come around.

My mother approaches me first. She is soft, beautiful, and smaller than I would have predicted. She offers me a luminous red glass heart and we hold each other for a long time. – Let me go, please. I will never really be gone, you know – . I don't want to let her go, but I do. She finds her door in the sky and the stars enfold her, closing the door behind her. I cry. My father approaches me last. – Child, you are so amazing and we will always be with you. With each breath, you honor your family, your heritage, your life. With each smile, you salute us on the other side. Know that you are whole and keep these gifts close to you. Here is my gift to you – . My father has made a lush cloak of ferns that he drapes around me gently, and then places a crown of flowers onto my head. He holds my face, looks at me with utter love, and smiles. He turns and walks to the star-scattered horizon and opens the door to the sky. He enters his tomb and it closes perfectly around him. One last great wave of sorrow washes through me and I hear the fern cloak whispering, grief-shaken. My tears cascade down the cloak and call forth flowers: there, a nasturtium; there, a morning glory; there, a lily. Tiny green frogs venture out of the fronds and let the moonlight wash over their smooth backs. Moths emerge and alight on flowers to drink nocturnal sweetness.

I gather the gifts of my ancestors into my arms and breathe. The glass heart of my mother becomes a real heart, *my heart, our heart,* and it beams joy through my whole body, extending through me and beyond me in a golden corona. At last, I am a Madonna, pregnant with the miracle of my own life force, gifted with all the necessary instruments for soul survival. I am free to hope for anything now, free to plant in the garden soil that once was filled only with bones.

# Deeper Still

*Grace Totherow*

From our perspective, she is fine. Right on time. The codes percolate inside her perfectly, an infusion of sacred geometry. She will achieve mastery. From our perspective, outside of time, she already has. She feels she is dragging, hanging by threads, shoulders heavy with dread and regret. From our perspective this is part of the process, the dross rising to the surface and burning away. These are the pangs of birth. She is entering a new world. She is a pillar of salt, sand, earth, crushed silver and bone, being honed by winds that shape her in immaculate curves and lines. The rains soften the stones imbedded in the folds of her mind. She is already home though her eyes search the horizon for signs showing the way.

You already know.

There is nowhere to go, child. We smile and wait for her to ask for help. We hover so close and though there are moments she can feel us, she mostly knows herself alone.

Go on. You can't do it wrong.

We are in awe of this human journey. From our perspective, your emotions are your greatest gift. The key to your destiny. There are many who envy you and this extraordinary opportunity to feel deeply. To embody the tones of eternity within each cell.

Let the sounds come through you. Let the new language spill from your lips. It's not new, really. It reverberates through the annals of time, reminding you of your origin. Your sounds will unlock all that is bound within the confines of space-time. You already know this story. In the beginning was the word. Your voices come forth in a chorus, amplifying a frequency that will resonate through this universe. Your dance is one of alchemy. Your heart knows the way. She beckons you gently into her ocean of stillness. Surrender, let go, tumble ever deeper, spinning inward. Shine your flashlight down the spiraling staircase of your own being. Shine the light of your own awareness on what you find and, when you've got your bearings, go deeper. You will discover there is nothing to fear.

When the ache is greatest, she believes she is failing, falling behind. We smile as she asks for guidance. We place a palm on her back. We lay a hand on her head and one over her heart. Her breath becomes even, her inner rhythm in sync.

We are not far away. We are here. Ask for help. Ask and you shall receive. You will achieve mastery. From our perspective, outside of time, you already have. Be at peace.

Illustration by Kathryn Sullivan

# The Magic Trick

*Aleks Stefanova*

To the Lion Sun that lives within me with its mouth gaping towards the stars above

To the fearful daemon that dreams of becoming a fearless God one day

To the gullible child ever so hopeful, ever so playful, ever so Life full

I give you my soul, a cup full of love, elevate it to a grateful toast

Thank you, ever so kindly, ever so greatly

You, a million knots threading the puzzle thread of this rug called my being

We as one are being present here together, for the flick of this flash called life

Never will we know the truth as a simple sentenced answer

Yet, always will we seek to shed a light to a greater purpose in the dark of this unique Magic Trick

Thank you, whoever you've been, whoever you are, whoever you become

To the strong of your strings, the twine that shapes you
Built you are to withstand the weight of this universe
Composed of a symphony that bears the key to change the way
this world dances
You are free to dare fearlessly, love passionately, you, my darling
Live life by the mouthful now and until the light fades

# WRITERS

When she's not floating at Float On, *S.H. Aeschliman* is at the Rocking Frog Cafe, writing prose and poetry (and prose poetry) about dusty heart-drawers, awkward sexual encounters, and being chased by nunchuck-wielding ducks. Under pseudonym she also writes romance and erotica with a strong social justice bent. Despite being a native Oregonian, she does not own a bicycle and is woefully under-prepared for the zombie apocalypse. She does, however, have an adorable dog named Milton – an Expert Urban Forager who helps her get through the dark days.

*Jane Belinda* is a queer poet from Portland, OR. They run an open mic and Slam called Slamlandia! They like to hang out with Douglas firs is their spare time and they are extremely mentally prepared for a 9.4 earthquake to hit the pacific northwest. They recently self-published a chapbook titled "Grief and Other Things Men Gave Me" about the pain that has come with their relationships with men. You can find more of their work at janebelinda.com

*Margot Bigg* is a freelance writer and editor specializing in travel, culture, and the arts. Her stories have appeared in publications around the world, including National Geographic

Traveller India, Rolling Stone India, VICE, Travel + Leisure, Slate, Sunset Magazine, Roads & Kingdoms, and The Oregonian. She's also the author of multiple guidebooks for Moon Guides and Fodor's. When not engaged in some combination of traveling and writing she enjoys reading, rock climbing, trail running, and standing on her head.

*Carly Jean Brynelson* is a Couples and Family Therapy Master's student (class of 2018) in Eugene, Oregon. Upon graduation, she hopes to collaborate with float centers and clinicians throughout the world to develop combined sensory deprivation, psychedelics, and counseling interventions for clients with complex PTSD. Her dream is to open and provide counseling services at a studio where clients float, use therapeutic psychedelics (if desired), and process their experiences with skillful counselors to expedite safe, transcendent, and effective healing journeys.

*Nikki Burian* is a 5th-century fragment of an illustration from an unknown work of literature. Nikki Burian is a lunar impact crater that is located within the huge walled plain of Apollo, on the far side of the Moon. Nikki Burian is a fossil from the Upper Devonian of Iowa. Nikki Burian is a toy that does some very weird things.

*Kiersi Burkhart* lives and works as an author and freelance writer in Wyoming. She co-authored the series QUARTZ CREEK RANCH for Middle-Grade readers, and is the sole author of the upcoming YA novel, HONOR CODE (Spring 2018). She grew up a cowgirl in Colorado and can still run a mean barrel race. While writing books and owning her own business, she still finds time to fight for justice and play Dungeons and Dragons on the weekends. She has a deep and abiding love of Pokemon, her husband, and her mutt Baby.

Satire Week Magazine has called *Greg Eldridge* an "indolent, hairy, intelligent-ape-man who whiles away the hours pondering what a while's worth while not doing much worthwhile." His nose hair has been described as "voluminously textured, reticulate yet granular," "spacious and layered," "apparitional," "cosmic and creative," "explores the relationship between Pre-Raphaelite tenets and counter terrorism." "With influences as diverse as Camus and Buckminster Fuller, new combinations of his nose hair are created from both opaque and transparent layers. As subtle replicas become transformed through boundaried and academic practice, the viewer is left with a tribute to the inaccuracies of our culture."

*Sarah Gallegos* participated in Float On's writer program in 2014.

*Phillip Hatcher* is an up and coming poet from Portland, Oregon. Growing up in the country and making a new life in the city, Phillip provides us with a humanistic view on modernity. Currently, he has his first collection out on sale entitled, "A Knife Through Static," which is a stitching of personal conflicts and views on a better quality of life.

*Dot Hearn* writes stories. True stories and fictionalized stories and fiction with dabs of truth. She believes in the cross-pollination of art and writing, of theatre and a creative life, of dancing and words on the page. Her published works include essays, poetry, short fiction, radio scripts, and creative nonfiction. Publications have included Hippocampus Magazine, Altopia Antholozine, Prism, Six Sentences, Hermana Resist's Voices Against Violence, Sudden Radio Project, and Blink Ink. She is currently working on a memoir, and a short story collection which has suddenly turned dystopian.

*Donovan James* is a writer, musician, and cat enthusiast. He is still an idealist, despite a ravaging cynicism. He believes that the money and effort allocated to war and fear should be used to feed, shelter, and educate the poor, no human being excluded. He's the author of the poetry collection "Saudade," and his work has appeared in Commonline Journal, Coldnoon Journal, aois21 Publishing, and Curious Apes. He has also written, acted, and directed plays for Monkey With A Hat On and Missing Link, Portland theater companies.

*Tasha Jamison* participated in Float On's Writing Program in 2015.

*Tanya Jarvik* deeply respects the subconscious mind's ability to generate compelling material. Her work has appeared in VoiceCatcher, The Manifest-Station, The Open Face Sandwich, the Enter at Your Own Risk anthology series, Marked by Scorn: An

Anthology Featuring Non-Traditional Relationships, and elsewhere. Tanya has taught composition, poetry, fiction, and memoir writing, and is currently a freelance editor and live storyteller. If asked to pinpoint her true calling in life, she would say it's somewhere near the intersection of stories and sex.

*Erick Mertz* participated in Float On's Writing Program in 2014.

*Andrew Nealon* was raised in Portland, Oregon, and enjoyed a public school education, where he focused on breaking the rules and challenging teachers. He went on to study film critique and emerging media theory in higher education for the better half of a decade at various institutions across America. Currently he is working in the worlds of music video, documentary, film, and television, as a sound technician & producer/director, taking periodic breaks to write & travel the world. He believes in a life filled with meditation and yoga to help unlock the body, mind, & spirit's natural gifts.

*Ben Ortlip* is originally from Levittown, Pennsylvania, and moved to the West Coast after a short stint in the US Air Force, where he monitored nuclear treaties and taught electronics. He graduated from The Evergreen State College with a focus in neuroscience and philosophy. He has been involved in the floatation community since 2012, and in 2013 helped to bring the first-ever working sensory deprivation tank to Burning Man. He has previously worked with Sound Photosynthesis and Samadhi Tank

Corporation, and currently lives in northern California, where he works as a house-sitter, freelance writer, and owner of www. antitrump.com.

*Steven Parton* is a programmer and author obsessed with exploring the depths of the human condition and technology, always with the end goal of promoting humanism. He likes to write stories that challenge his readers to examine cultural and philosophical issues through immersive and exciting world-building. He believes there is nothing more important than cultivating self while loving all that life brings your way, but that one should never forget to laugh either. When not writing, he enjoys biking, traveling, philosophizing, and partaking in food and cheer.

*Ken Pico* is a native San Diegan whose love for the written word blossomed early and who found an outlet for his voice through local, weekly news publications and summer writing programs in high school. Having tired of "the endless summer" nearly a decade ago, he feels right at home in the PNW. In recent years, he has dabbled in slam poetry and in local open mics and is currently focused on compiling his poetry into a sequence of chapbooks. He lives in northeast Portland with his panther-of-a-cat Aden and owns and operates the Rocking Frog Café in Portland's Buckman neighborhood.

*Rooze* works across multiple medias and genres and often spills one onto the other. Their poetry and photography has been published in (em): a Review of Text and Image, American Tanka,

Anatomy and Etymology, Cabildo Quarterly, Raven Chronicles, World Haiku, and on the cover of Carve Magazine. Rooze received a BFA in Creative Writing from Goddard College and an MFA in Creative Writing from Stonecoast (University of Southern Maine) and currently lives in Portland, Oregon with their partner and incredibly spoiled cats, Harry and Pippa. For more information, visit roozecentral.com.

*C. Starling* is a fiction writer, bookkeeper, knitter, and cocktail enthusiast. She started floating in an attempt to help muscle spasms caused by long-term stress and anxiety, and it took a few tries before she was able to really give in to the process. Her time in the floating program helped her relax - and get over her fear of the dark!

*Aleks Stefanova* lives in Portland Oregon and finds poetry to be a very therapeutic art form. She writes whenever she hears the call and works her day job otherwise. She has been a regular participant in the Portland Poetry Slam and was an organizer for Awkward Open Mic. She is also the creator of Q Poetry, a queer poetry network. Her performances can be found on youtube, and she can be reached at astefanova@hotmail.com.

*Michele Steward* is a local model, mom, crafter and float-lover living in Portland, OR.

*K.C. James Swain* was born and raised in Portland, Oregon. He is a writer, husband, cat lover, podcaster, photo booth attendant, classic Chevy truck owner, adventurer, food lover, former college athlete and storyteller. He is the author of a book of poetry titled, Open Letter to the Man. Currently, K.C. is working towards a Master of Science in Education at Portland State University to be a high school language arts teacher.

Since graduating with a BA in Dance in 2001 from Hollins University, *Grace Totherow* has been deeply involved in the performing arts. She's been a creative writing mentor to teens and children, traveled throughout the west in a gypsy wagon playing music, and directed dance theater projects in rural Utah. She created her first one-woman show, "Star and Stone," in 2013. She is currently studying to become an American Sign Language/English interpreter.

You'll find *Courtney Watson* spending her time diving into the vast inner spaces of Self, as well as helping others find the courage to do the same. She spends her days assisting women in rediscovering their wild intuition and tapping into their creative cycles. In her personal life, Courtney seeks inspiration from her own ebbs and flows, allowing the words to offer alternative perspectives of existence.

*Ken Yoshikawa* is a poet, actor, and astrologer from Portland, OR. He loves his friends and family. He finds that in order to make battle with oppression it is important to respect science, believe in magic and listen to women. That last one sounds bizarre, but it really is possible. Floating for him is a useful tool to navigate the particularly monstrous path to his center. This pairs well with writing poetry, which cracks the bat on evil Dr. Apathy and the eternal trolls of existential dread. You can find him online under the handle of Yo Shake Awaken.

# ILUSTRATORS

*Liliya Dru* is an illustrator and graphic designer whose focus is on feminism and ecology. See more of her work on LiliyaDru.com.

*Levi Greenacres* is a tattooer, author, and illustrator in Portland, Oregon. Levi is 20% country gravy, 48% dream journal, 23% ink pen, and 0% math. Many of his words and pictures are at www.levigreenacres.com, and on social media @levigreenacres.

*Mike Skrzynski* is an illustrator, designer, photographer, and multimedia artist originally hailing from California. He originally ventured to Portland 20+ years ago to go to college. He decided to stay, and since then has been honing his skills in the media arts. He is currently most focused on comics and illustration.

*Kathryn Sullivan* has a massive callus on her ring finger from the hard metal of her tablet pc digitizer. She's always drawing. She's always been drawing. She draws float tanks for a living, and fine vellus hairs for fun.

# ACKNOWLEDGEMENTS

There is a very good chance this book would not have been completed without the help of my good friend and co-editor Sione Aeschliman. Not only did she put in an enormous amount of the legwork getting this collection of writings turned into a book, she also introduced me to a rich vein of talented writers who really breathed new life into the project. That is not to minimize the contribution of the other writers who came to hear about the program through other means. Thanks to the owners of Float On, Graham Talley, Ashkahn Jahromi, Jake Marty, Christopher Messer, and Quinn Zepeda for welcoming me into this strange, dark, and salty business of and giving me the freedom to do weird projects like making this book. Big thanks to Josh Fitz for the editing and formatting and Kathryn Sullivan for creating the cover art. Thank you to the staff of Float On for keeping the tanks running and the floaters happy. Thank you to the late John C. Lilly, Jay Shurley, and the past and current giants of the float world. And of course thank you to all of the writers and illustrators who contributed to this book.

—Marshall Hammond

# Letters from the Void

The typeface used in this book is Aldus, designed by Hermann Zapf in 1954—the same year as the first float tank.

Design & Composition by Graham Talley
and Josh Fitz in Portland, OR.

Manufactured in the United States of America.

Coincidence Control Publishing
4530 SE Hawthorne Blvd
Portland, OR 97215

Made in the USA
San Bernardino, CA
03 August 2017